AGENT 009
SOME NIGHTS GET CHILLY

PART 1 OF 3

Jerry Calonge

TABLE OF CONTENTS

Act 1
Introduction
to
Langichatte LaBond

CHAPTER 1
A WARM WELCOME

FBI Special Operations Briefing Room, Miami, Florida 04:00 AM, Local Time

The hum of fluorescent lights buzzed overhead like a nervous mosquito trapped in bureaucracy. A half-eaten donut sat sweating under the heat lamp on a table that hadn't been wiped down since the Obama administration. The air was thick with anticipation, stale coffee, and the scent of old leather from chairs that had seen too many failed missions and too few promotions.

Agent Gil Arenas, the original first double 0, dressed in his freshly pressed tactical suit, stood before a wall-sized digital screen displaying satellite imagery of a mega-yacht the size of a minor country. The vessel gleamed in the moonlight like a Bond villain's vacation rental. Stenciled in pretentious gold on the side of the boat: "The Narcotic Dream."

Yeah, subtlety wasn't exactly ZoGod's thing.

"Alright, everyone. Eyes up, mouths shut," Agent Arenas said, clicking a button on his tablet. The screen flickered to an infrared view of the yacht. Dozens of heat signatures in police boat have completely surrounded this over-the-top monstrosity. Ready to receive the signal, so, they can move in and catch the bad guy. Like a game of Where's Waldo if Waldo were packing heat and bags of uncut Bolivian party powder.

"This is not a drill, people. Operation Narcotic Dream is a go."

The room went still. Half a dozen agents leaned forward. One dropped his phone but made a show of pretending it was intentional.

Agent Arenas paced like a caffeinated general. "We've tracked Jean-Paul Joseph, a.k.a. ZoGod, for the past fourteen months. We've hit him four times. FOUR." He held up four fingers like he was counting sins. "And every time, he's slipped through our hands like an oiled eel in a silk suit."

The agents nodded grimly. It was true. ZoGod was a ghost wrapped in swag. His last known location had been a private island he bought using cryptocurrency and five gym bags of cash, all C-notes, from his illegal ventures. His Instagram account was still posting beach-side flexing selfies, though they suspected it was run by an intern.

Agent Arenas clicked again. The screen zoomed in on a man in a crimson velvet robe standing on the yacht's helipad.

"That's our guy," Arenas said. "Third-most wanted on the Bureau's list. Narcotics trafficking. Weapons smuggling. Hosting an illegal underground fashion show that may or may not have included a tiger."

One of the younger agents, Agent Ben, raised his hand. "Is that the one where the models were also weapons dealers?"

Arenas sighed. "Yes…" as he looks directly at agent Ben "but not all the models were in on it. It was our first attempt to catch ZoGod. I was undercover that day. I met these two beautiful models named Samaya and Valouna… their sexy legs still hunt my dreams like I was John himself, in -Threefold Desire. But anyway…" As he turned to face his team. "The tiger wore sunglasses… this guy took us for a joke for far too long. And if the tiger is there too. I want his butt to get arrested for being an accomplice. All he's little games will end today."

There was a moment of solemn silence as the agents contemplated the sheer gall of it all.

"Now, we've got our inside man Agent Curtis. He just confirmed that the buy is going down in fifty minutes. Weapons in exchange for products. It's a major handoff, and we're going to be there when the hammer drops."

Arenas tapped the screen again, bringing up a tactical map of the Florida Keys, overlaid with routes and agent placement.

"We've got eyes in the sky two Black Hawks and one sneaky drone named Sharon. We've got the Coast Guard on standby and a water blockade tighter than my Aunt Cheryl's Tupperware. Within seven minutes from the time of our arrival, no one will be able to escape."

"I don't want to rain on your parade boss" agent Ben yelled out. "I mean, we've got Black Hawks, drones, and a Tupperware-air tight blockade. But what if, and please, bear with me, by us trying to arrest him in seven minutes, he escapes in six minutes through a submarine like he did last time... mind blowing to think about... right?"

"No, no, no... no one could escape in 6 minutes"

"I'm just saying, he can have another submarine."

Arenas' eye twitched.

"No submarine," he said, through gritted teeth. "no one can really escape in six minutes; we will lock everything up in seven cause that's the magic number. but just in case, he

can be like mission impossible and do it in six. we've accounted for that. Thermal tracking, and an actual guy named Rick who just stares at the water all day trust me. We've got it."

A collective murmur of satisfaction rumbled through the room.

Then, just to hammer it home, Arenas leaned in, his voice a gravelly whisper.

"This guy tried to smuggle meth disguised as baby powder. He's a menace. A manipulator. He once convinced an entire nightclub in Dubai that he was Jay-Z's cousin and left with three yachts and a camel. We can't afford another screw-up. Are we clear?"

"Yes, sir!" came the chorus.

"Good. Then let's do this by the book. By the numbers. By the god-damn Constitution of the United States… itself, do you all hear me?"

"Sir, yes Sir" the entire chorus were eager to prove their worth.

"But I need this so-called Zo of God arrested today."

One of the agents accidentally saluted.

Arenas clicked the tablet one last time, bringing up a live aerial feed of the yacht rocking gently on the moonlit ocean.

"All units deploy. I want that boat wrapped tighter than that mansion with those ten thousand cases of baby oils. This is ZoGod's last chapter."

The room exploded into motion.

Boots hit the floor. Kevlar was zipped. Guns were checked. Radios crackled.

Agents poured out of the briefing room like an ant swarm in tactical black. Sirens flicked to life on blacked-out SUVs that peeled out of the FBI motor pool like they were auditioning for Fast & Furious: Federal Files.

Inside one of the vehicles, Agent Arenas buckled up and turned to his partner, Agent Carmichael, a woman who could arm-wrestle a bull and make it apologize afterward as she addresses him.

"You think this is finally it?".

Arenas smirked. "If it's not, I'm gonna personally fly to wherever he disappears next, dip my whole body in honey and slap his tiger."

Off the Florida Coast – The Narcotic Dream

Time: 04:40 AM

The Atlantic lay still under a blanket of predawn fog, the ocean a mirror to the heavens if the heavens had a thing for smuggling.

Out in open waters, isolated like a millionaire's fever dream, floated The Narcotic Dream. A mega-yacht the size of a football field, hand designed with ZoGod unique taste. The hull gleamed with an obsidian sheen, its chrome trim catching the moonlight like the edge of a villain's dagger. Neon-blue under-lights cast an ominous glow beneath the surface, attracting curious fish and repelling curious authorities.

Onboard, silence reigned.

But not the suspenseful, string-quartet-on-the-verge-of-tragedy kind. No. This was an awkward, "everyone here is pretending they're not criminals but are" kind of silence.

On the edge of the back of the yacht, five mercenaries ex-KGB, two former UFC rejects, and one guy who claimed to be a monk until Tuesday but most people know him as Twitchy Forkan. Four of those men sat around, pretending to fish, holding their fish rods, and liquor and cigars in their other hands. Beautiful women were everywhere on the boat. The other four men were playing poker with ZoGod, using some of the women as chips.

Bets were set

As cards were tossed

And winners were made

The winner got to kiss all the losers' girls' lips, or laid on her breast, or kiss their butts. And the so-called monk aka Twitchy Forkan was having a hell of a lucky day as most of the good cards kept on landing in his favor.

It was all fun and games. This was their normal after party, after a night of fun and clubbing.

Jean-Paul Joseph, seated like a god among men, legs crossed, robe flowing in the sea breeze, AKA ZoGod. Haitian-born, globally-feared, charisma leaking from his pores like the rum in his platinum cocktail glass. Haitian rum 5-star Barbancourt.

He lounged in a crimson velvet armchair, the kind you'd expect to see in a villain's therapy office. The glass in his hand shimmered a radioactive shade of green-blue, the cocktail's recipe probably illegal in most countries due to the party drugs mix in the rum. Enough to get a buzz but not enough to serve real time in jail.

Atop his perfectly waxed chest, glistening with tropical oils, sat a full-color tattoo of himself shirtless, of course riding a dolphin with a gold chain and sunglasses. The dolphin was mid-leap. The tattoo had shading. Someone paid real money for this.

ZoGod lifted his wrist, press a button on his diamond-encrusted smartwatch, the sound of helicopters up a head. Without even looking up, said in a voice that sounded like smooth jazz soaked in menace:

"Get ready boys. They're coming."

The voice that responded came from a hidden speaker embedded in a seashell-shaped dome above his head. The yacht had over 200 hidden speakers. Most were playing a continuous loop of 90s hip-hop instrumentals mix with Haitian music. This one was for business.

Disembodied Voice (Gravelly, deep Haitian accent):

"We're ready boss. All perimeters are lock, and all exits are sealed. And I personally told Ti-Jacko to hide the caviar in a decoy container labeled 'dog food.' We're prepared, sir."

ZoGod didn't smile so much as purr. His eyes remained closed, head tilted back to absorb the moonlight like it was charging his ego. But the statement that come from the intercom had him confused.

"Wait, why did you nitwits had to relabel the caviar? You know what, never mind. Agent Gil and the alphabet boys are coming. Let's just have some fun."

He lifted his drink, sipped with God-tier arrogance, then added:

"And tell the tiger to get the GoPro ready."

There was a pause on the line.

Disembodied Voice:

"You mean your tiger, Sir?"

ZoGod: "No. The other one. Of course, my tiger stupid. Who's in the bridge right now, is that Ti-Ruby,"

"Yes sir." Ti-Ruby replied.

"Ti-Ruby where's Captain Alex?"

"It's Captain Alex Millien's day off Sir. I'm filling in for him, as the acting Captain, Sir."

"An acting captain who never had a boat. So, you wanna play captain on my boat. Listen to me stupid, don't touch nothing up there, don't even use the telecommunication system again… unless it's very important. Do I make myself clear… you nitwit."

"Yes… s. s. s. sir…" Scared half to death, Ti-Ruby reluctantly replied.

He snapped his fingers twice, and from the shadows emerged Shamgod, a full-grown Bengal tiger wearing an ivory harness fitted with a GoPro, two tactical pouches, and what looked suspiciously like a small custom-made earpiece.

The tiger padded over, nuzzled ZoGod's knee, then turned to face the rising sun like, it too, had a vendetta.

ZoGod: "Good boy. Let's immortalize this moment. I want the footage cut together with slo-mo, string music, and at least three reaction shots of me looking annoyed but powerful."

A smaller figure appeared behind ZoGod: Momo, his 17-year-old social media manager unpaid intern, former coding prodigy, and unwilling hostage.

Momo: "Sir, just a reminder… we're banned on YouTube. Also, the footage from the last operation got flagged for 'extreme violence, fashion violations, and misuse of a tiger.'"

ZoGod (still staring into the horizon):

"Then post it on TikTok. And set it to something iconic. Like Tabou Combo Lakay. Or Joé-Dwet Filé Fem Voyé."

Momo: "Right…"

Behind them, another mercenary approached, helmet in hand. He was sweating through his bulletproof Armani.

Mercenary: "Boss, final system checks complete. Drone jammers are online. Anti-sub sensors are pinging like crazy. We even picked up a dolphin that looked suspicious, but he swam away."

ZoGod: "That's because dolphins have a conscience. Unlike our guests."

He stood now, slowly. Grandly. Robe fluttering behind him like a comic book cape. His feet bare on teak wood polished to military standards. He walked to the edge of the yacht, gazing out over the water with theatrical reverence.

ZoGod: "They'll come thinking they have the upper hand. Thinking this is their story. Their mission. But I say this to you "

He turned, holding his glass aloft like a chalice.

"This is my movie."

A beat passed. The wind blew his robe open for a moment; he was wearing a man thong. No one dared react.

Shamgod growled approvingly.

Momo clapped once. Half-heartedly

FBI Motorcade, Approaching Miami Dockside

The convoy tore through the streets of Miami like a government-funded stampede. Dozens of black SUVs with tinted windows swerved onto the shipping port's entrance ramp, their tires screaming against the pavement. Floodlights swept across the coastline like spotlights on a red carpet only this carpet was made of salt, sweat, and the scent of diesel.

Agent Gil Arenas' SUV led the charge. He slammed the brakes hard, his vehicle screeching to a halt at the edge of the port. He stepped out and took in the view.

An FBI helicopter was already waiting for him. ZoGod's yacht could be seen from those distances surrounded by police boats with red and blue lights illuminating the early

morning darkness. Ahead of him, the docks rose like a maze of steel and secrets. Agent Gil Arenas and his partner agent Carmichael run past a container and got into the helicopter with agent Ben by their side.

Arenas narrowed his eyes. "Tom is going to finally catch Jerry." he muttered.

ZoGod: "Begin the playlist."

Instantly, the yacht's speakers blared to life with 'Bon Feeling by Haitian-American female artist Dajé. It echoed across the ocean like the arrival of divine irony.

ZoGod: "Now… let's greet our uninvited guests."

Three dozen of tactical agents poured out of the surrounding police boats climbing ZoGod mega yacht, like a black-clad SWAT ballet. Weapons were drawn. Headsets clicked into place. Eyes scanned every shadow. As agent Arenas' helicopter landed on the helipad, ZoGod was there, ready to greet him.

As agent Arenas step out, he looks at agent Ben "Like I said seven minutes was the key. Look at him, he has nowhere to go."

"Or, maybe he wasn't trying to run away, sir." Agent Ben replied. Agent Arenas look at agent Ben with discontent. And was ready to give him a dagger of a reply, but ZoGod screamed broke the tension. "My brother Gil, welcome. It's been too long since we last seen each other, face to face."

Arenas "Trust me when I tell you, the pleasure is not mine. And when I place a shiny new jewelry on your wrist. It won't be yours either." As he raised his two-way radio to his lips.

Arenas: "All units, comb through every deck and every corner… now, do you copy!"

Silence.

He frowned. "Bravo-team, I repeat... search the damn boat."

Nothing but a low hiss of static.

Arenas looked around. "Bravo-team, respond. I repeat Bravo-team, do you copy?"

His radio flickered. Buzzed.

"Come on brotha Gil, you came all this way to visit me and you thought I'm going to take it easy on you?"

(Radio still Distorted): agent Arenas turns to agent Ben

"Go tell the team to search the entire place. And you go turn off whatever is jamming our communication system, now."

"Let see your divine powers" agent Arenas barked. "You're surrounded. We've got a warrant. This is your last chance to cooperate, and just maybe, we will place an end date to your sentence."

ZoGod reeled one of the fishing lines with dramatic flair, looking at agent Arenas dead in the eyes.

"Don't feel bad, brotha Gil. I, too, have spent my life trying to catch a big white shark. Still haven't caught one. Story of my life."

Agent Arenas didn't smile.

Two snow bunnies' approach ZoGod's strode out from below deck in matching white bikinis, each holding a martini. One kissed ZoGod's cheek; the other offered him a cigar. He took it, lit it, and exhaled slowly.

Moments later, agents fanned out across the yacht, opening every drawer, checking compartments, running swabs and scans.

"Control, this is Bravo Team," came a voice over comms. "No drugs, no weapons, no contraband. The yacht is clean."

Agent Arenas' jaw clenched.

ZoGod turned to face him fully now, arms wide. "As you can see, I'm just a simple man... trying to catch fish and feelings." His entourage chuckled in the background.

Agent Ben shoved past the girls, growling, "This is bull"

"Stand down," agent Arenas interrupted. "We're done here."

As the last agents disembarked, ZoGod gave them a mock salute, then returned to his fishing rod with the confidence of a man who just won a game he never agreed to play.

Back onshore, a younger agent pulled up drone footage on a tablet. "Sir... we've got movement at Safehouse 7."

The screen zoomed in on a shark-infested pool an unofficial part of ZoGod's security system. Inside the water, the shapes of three large bull sharks circled lazily. Between them floated torn pieces of black wetsuit, bone fragments, and a bloodied human leg.

Everyone watching the feed went silent.

"Curtis," agent Ben whispered. "That's our undercover agent."

"If it was bullets, he probably coulda have a chance to live. But those sharks' bit him nine times. He can't spit out nothing, they're already digesting."

A gust of wind carried ZoGod's laughter from across the water.

"We can go back and arrest him right now," junior agent Ben said, already gripping his weapon.

But field commander agent Gil Arenas shook his head. "No. He's clean again. He's always two steps ahead."

"Then what the hell do we do?"

The commander stared at the bloody water one last time.

"We stop thinking like agents.

And start thinking outside the box."

Port-au-Prince, Haiti

Time: 9:17 AM

An old man was brushing his dentures.

He stood in front of a mirror hung askew in a dimly lit bathroom where every tile told a story, and each crack whispered of earthquakes and old age. The dentures squeaked under the bristles like they were protesting the early wake-up call. When he finished, he clicked them into his mouth with the satisfaction of a man locking in a cheat code.

Old Man:

"Time to walk my chicken," he said proudly, staring at himself in the mirror with the authority of a general preparing for war.

He slipped on a floral-print shirt, basketball shorts that had never seen a court, and a pair of sandals with more personality than most Instagram influencers. He turned toward the living room.

"Frédéric! Where are you at, my feathered warrior?"

From behind the couch emerged a chicken. But not just any chicken. Frédéric had swagger. A bright red comb that flopped slightly like a greaser's pompadour and a gait like he knew he owned the block. Around his neck: a leather dog collar with "BOSS" spelled out in rhinestones.

The old man crouched and clipped a leash to the collar.

"Let's stretch our legs, boy. Sun's hot, but not as hot as my hips after a morning run."

He opened the front door, stepped onto the sun-drenched stoop, and began his daily routine walking Frédéric through the narrow streets of Port-au-Prince like it was Central Park, and they were royalty.

"Bonjou, Misye Baptiste!"

"Morning, Chicken King!"

Locals greeted him with laughter and fondness. Frédéric puffed his feathers in response, pecking at the occasional pebble and strutting like he was born for this.

But someone was watching.

Across the street, leaning against a cracked lamppost in the shadows of a faded billboard for a Haitian toothpaste brand, stood a man in ragged clothing.

His beard was overgrown. His shirt said "ONOV Cause my Voice Matter" in a font printed in a hurry. His eyes tracked the chicken's every movement like a hawk on Red Bull.

He stepped into the sun, cracking his knuckles.

Stranger (muttering):

"That's the one. That's the chicken that'll change it all."

Meanwhile – Just Two Blocks Away

Langichatte LaBond adjusted the angle of his straw fedora, letting it catch just enough sun to make his skin glow. He stood in the middle of a bustling open-air market in Port-au-Prince, surrounded by honking tap-taps, shouting vendors, clucking chickens, and the smell of grilled plantains mingled with engine smoke.

A legend in his linen. Langichatte LaBond always dress to impress. You can find him almost every week in Richard Store in Pétion-Ville.

Dressed in a button up white short-sleeve shirt with a backward tie, pressed khaki three-quarter pants, dress shoes with white socks, and enough swagger to start his political party, Langichatte moved through the market like he owned the heat.

"Madam Tatee!" he called, spotting a peanut vendor. "Still here, poisoning people with your delicious addiction?"

The old woman barked a laugh. "Langichatte! You disrespect me and compliment me in the same breath. You trying to confuse my menopause?"

Langichatte popped a peanut in his mouth. "Your peanuts are the reason people fall in love, then lose everything."

"Not my fault if love makes fools," she said, handing him a small bag.

He took it without paying. "Add it to my tab."

"You already owe me enough to buy a car."

"I'll pay in charm. I've got surplus."

He strolled further, tossing peanuts into his mouth one by one, glancing around like a secret agent looking for danger but mostly just admiring his city.

"Look at this place," he said, to no one in particular. "This is real paradise. Not that American concrete jungle they call Miami. Have you ever seen joy like this in cold weather?"

A fruit vendor nearby chimed in. "But America got opportunity."

"Opportunity to freeze your soul!" Langichatte replied. "That cold air? That's the weather of villains. If your breath turns white when you talk, maybe God's trying to tell you to shut up."

A ripple of laughter moved through the market.

Langichatte turned slowly, opened his arms wide, and gestured to the sky. "Here, we got heat, heart, and hustle. Do you know what happens when you move to those cold countries? People are walking around, like their knees owe them money!"

Just then, the air shifted.

A sudden shout interrupted the comedy routine.

"Thief! Thief! Thief! Stop him… He stole my chicken!"

Heads turned as Mr. Baptiste stood by an ice cream cart, his arms flailing in disbelief. "My chicken! My boy Frédéric! Somebody stop him!"

A blur shot past Langichatte.

The Chicken Thief sprinted through the crowd with the tied-up bird in his arms, head down, dodging pedestrians like a madman.

Langichatte handed the peanut bag to a small child.

"Hold this bag for me. But if I come back and it's empty, I'll know you have good taste."

Then he took off.

The market erupted into chaos.

Vendors ducked.

Chickens squawked. A woman screamed and threw a bottle of hot sauce for no reason.

The Chicken Thief crashed through a rack of T-shirts, leaving a cloud of dust and misplaced slogans behind. Langichatte hurdled over a goat and skidded across a fruit crate.

"IN THE NAME OF THE LAW, I ORDER YOU TO STOP!" he bellowed, arms windmilling wildly.

The thief darted through an alley, vaulted over a pile of tires, and leapt into a backyard garden.

Langichatte followed without hesitation, crashing into a wheelbarrow, launching a rain of cabbages into the sky.

The thief knocked over a fruit stand. Langichatte leapt over it barely. Bananas flew. People screamed. The thief dashed into a residential courtyard. Langichatte followed, crashing through the front gate, accidentally kicking over a flower pot that rolled into a dog's bowl. The dog barked. Langichatte barked back.

The chase spiraled into a house under renovation. The thief vaulted over a couch. Langichatte hurled a cushion after him, missed completely, and broke a lamp in the process.

The thief hurled a chair behind him. Langichatte ducked and crashed through a window instead, rolling onto a pile of laundry.

Boom.

Dust. Splinters. Regret.

"Zaboka mwen!" screamed someone from inside.

Langichatte dusted himself off and kept running. The thief jumped over a fence. Langichatte kicked open the gate like a Haitian Rambo with a badge and a grudge.

Finally, the thief ran out of breath and turned to Langichatte.

Panting. Sweating. Cornered.

"Okay... okay. Officer please, why are you chasing me and my pet chicken."

"Cause you're a chicken thief. That chicken doesn't belong to you."

"What a disrespectful thing to say, are you trying to call me a thief? HeyheyHey! This is my pet chicken."

"If this is your pet chicken, then, what is his name?"

"You think you're asking me some type of trick question or something. My pet chickens name issss... Delicious."

Langichatte raised an eyebrow. "You gave your pet chicken the name Delicious?"

"Yes, officer. My chicken is gender neutral."

Langichatte stared at him for a long beat, while grabbing the chicken from him. Then he walked ten steps away, placed the chicken gently on the ground, and turned to the thief. "Call your pet. Let's see if Delicious knows his daddy. Cause if he doesn't come know that I will not only arrest you for stealing a chicken but I will also arrest you for insulting my intelligence."

The thief cleared his throat and panic fills his heart. "Delicious! Come here, boy! Delicious, please come to me, daddy Delly don't want to go to jail. Delicious! come to me!"

The chicken blinked at him. Scratched its feathers. Wandered off in the opposite direction.

"Yeah. That's what I thought. Turn around, you're under arrest."

But the chicken thief Delly raised one hand, palm out.

"I see, you want to be a hero. But before we throw hands," he said solemnly, "let me speak my truth."

Langichatte blinked. "What the Sweet Micky?"

The thief stepped into the shade, hands folded.

"I'm a kung fu master," he began, as if testifying in church. "You see… a long time ago, I had a major gambling habit. Dice. Cards. Roosters. If it could lose money, I bet on it."

Langichatte looked around. "Is this a motivational speech or do you still want this beatdown?"

"Shh," the thief said, eyes misting. "I lost everything my wife, my kids, my house. Even my dignity. I've been living on the streets, surviving off boiled corn and regret. I don't gamble anymore... but I needed this chicken. This is my comeback. One last bet. This chicken wins, I get my wife back and become the best daddy to my two baby girls. Arley and Arhiana. I built a home. So, I can make love to my wife again and she can give birth to my third daughter, I would name her, Sahajlee. Maybe I even find God."

He squared his shoulders.

"I'm sorry I stole it. But I have to do this. So, I'm giving you a chance to walk away now. Or, I'll beat you from trying to stop me from stealing."

Langichatte crossed his arms. "You don't have enough balls in your pants to beat me."

The thief dropped into a deep horse stance and shouted: "I am a 9th-degree 7th-degree black belt. I suggest you walk away now before I kick your butt. No Diddy."

Langichatte snorted. "That sentence alone deserves a beating."

And the thief attacked.

With a sudden, loud "HI-YA!" he sprang forward, delivering a flying side kick that Langichatte barely dodged by stumbling back. The thief landed with surprising grace, following up with a chain of fast palm strikes. Langichatte blocked the first, ducked the second but the third slapped him right across the sunglasses.

"Oof!"

He staggered.

The thief grinned and pivoted into a spinning crescent kick that clipped Langichatte on the shoulder, sending him tumbling over a trash bin. Plastic bottles are scattered everywhere.

Langichatte sat up, dazed.

"You trained at TrendCatch Advertising Dojo?" he muttered. "Cause that 99 dollars you paid per month, may get you lots of clients from advertising but it will never give you the kung fu skills to beat me."

"That's what you think. You're going to find out who, Chicken Thief Delly really is."

Chicken Thief Delly didn't let up. He lunged forward again, unleashing an exaggerated crane-style stance one leg up, arms flapping like wings. Then he struck with rapid jabs that came with sound effects he made himself:

"PAP pwow! PAP pwow! Mom mwow!"

Langichatte tried to block but got jabbed in the ribs.

"Okay," he gasped. "You got rhythm. I respect that."

Then came the elbow strikes. Chicken Thief Delly spun in a wide circle, landed two shots to Langichatte's chest, and performed a backflip over a stray bench just because he could.

Langichatte rolled to the side, panting. "Alright. Enough."

He slowly reached down, unbuckled his belt with the care of a samurai unsheathing his ancestral blade.

"You made me mad. Now I'm going to make you call 911 like Wyclef."

The leather slid free from the loops with a hiss. Langichatte gripped it tightly.

Chicken Thief Delly paused, eyes narrowing. "A belt?"

Langichatte flicked his wrist.

The belt cracked through the air like thunder.

Chicken Thief Delly's confidence wavered slightly, as he moves his body and place himself in a different karate style. "Okay... who you think you're going to beat with this belt, your son. I'm a grown man."

Langichatte stepped forward, slowly.

"Have you ever been beaten with love, seasoning, and responsibility at the same time?"

"Never, but I would love to see you try." Chicken Thief Delly attacked first again a jab to the stomach.

Langichatte blocked it with the coiled belt. The leather absorbed the strike with a slap, then whipped around then hit Thief Delly's butt with the belt. Instantly Thief Delly's eyes watered. Overpowering Fear begin to speak to him in English. "Run my Zoe, Run. What's in from of you right now is a Super Unc. Zoe. One hit and you already have flashback about your dad. And your Dad been dead for 14 years now. This is not a fight you want my Zoe. Unc. must be a notch better than you. He must be a 9th-degree 8th-degree black belt. You better Run!" Confused and defiant Thief Delly place himself in a new karate stance, while his legs wanted to run. His last remaining 15 % of courage he had left took back control, as he scream back to himself. "I don't understand what you're saying to me. How can my thoughts speak to me in English? Palé Creole."

Then Thief Delly turns to langichatte "I'm not afraid of you." Langichatte spun, dragging him sideways into a barrel of rotting mangoes.

SPLAT.

"Ow-wwww!" Thief Delly shouted, emerging sticky and dazed.

Langichatte advanced. The belt snapped forward like a whip, striking his head, shoulder, knees and toes. "Ow, my knees and toes." Chicken Thief Delly painfully cried out. Every strike came with a sound of discipline: SMACK. WHACK. SNAP.

Thief Delly tried to rush in. Langichatte twirled the belt like a helicopter blade, deflecting a roundhouse, then catching Chicken Thief Delly's leg mid-kick.

The thief flipped sideways into a crate of empty bottles.

CRASH!

A crowd began to gather, whispering, recording on phones.

One man shouted, "That's Langichatte! He's using The Belt!"

"I heard the last guy he gave a butt whooping to, change his life and became a dentist. Now he gets free dental care for life." Another replied.

Thief Delly scrambled up, groaning, trying his best to make Langichatte feel bad. "In America, you would be arrested for hitting your kids with a belt as a form of punishment."

Langichatte smirked. "So lucky for me, were not in America. And you're not my kid."

Thief Delly swung wildly. Langichatte ducked, looped the belt over his neck not choking, just enough to guide him like a goat on a leash and flung him forward into a drying clothesline. Undergarments flew everywhere.

Then Langichatte reeled him back in.

"I call this move: 'Bring your butt here.'"

He yanked the belt again. Thief Delly stumbled forward, and Langichatte delivered a clean back-elbow to the nose.

CRACK.

Then grab Thief Delly from the back of his collar and begin to give him a butt whooping with his belt. "didn I tell you if you insult my intelligence I'm gonna make you pay."

Oui papa, oui papa, I'm sorry papa, please papa! I'm sorry papa!" As Thief Delly's butt gets redder and redder.

"You thought I was joking with you?"

"Non papa."

"Trust me, that butt whooping I just gave you, hurt me more than it hurts you. You're under arrest.

Back at the police station, Langichatte entered like he was returning from war. One hand held Chicken Thief Delly in cuffs, the other held a bucket of steaming fried chicken.

The lobby erupted.

Vendors from the market, residents from the houses, random bystanders who had witnessed the chaos and their properties getting damage by Langichatte all were there, yelling and pointing fingers. Papers flew. Someone screamed something about a broken toilet. While police officers are holding them at bay.

Captain Conrad stepped out of his office, eyes bulging.

"Langichatte! What the hell happened out there?!"

Langichatte placed the bucket of chicken on the desk and calmly sat Chicken Thief Delly down on a bench.

"I caught the chicken thief, Captain. You're welcome."

"You destroyed half the neighborhood! Just so you can catch a chicken thief?"

"But justice was served. With a side of drumsticks."

"Where did you even get that chicken?" the elderly owner, Monseieur Baptiste stepped forward, eyeing the bucket suspiciously. "That's not Frédéric, is it?"

Langichatte looked offended. "Do you see the word 'KFC' written on this bucket?"

"No," the old man Baptiste replied slowly.

"Exactly. This chicken came from... uh... local sources."

"It looks like my chicken!"

Langichatte leaned in. "Your chicken's name was Frédéric, right?"

"Yes!"

He held up a crispy wing. "Then this is not your chicken. This one's name is Alfredo."

Captain Conrad Laurore buried his face in his hands.

Before he could respond, the office phone rang.

The captain picked up. "Station de Police de Port-au-Prince."

Static.

"Hello? Hello? Oui? Yes, I can hear you. Who is this?"

More static. A deep American voice cut through in broken segments.

"...US. Intelligence... requesting... best field agent... urgent"

"What? What did you say? You need what?"

"...best agent... your most reliable..."

The captain squinted at the phone. "You want my worst agent, my most unreliable? That's an odd request but who am I to tell you no."

"...No, no no-we said best"

"I understand. My worst agent. I'll send him right away."

"Wait, no!"

Click.

Captain Conrad Laurore turned slowly toward Langichatte, who was now licking his fingers and teasing a drumstick at the thief.

"Today is my lucky day, the Good Lord finally smiles upon me, I prayed and prayed to God, to get a reprieve from you and today, He finally answered… oh, thank you Jesus, thank you Jesus, thank you Jesus," the captain said with a thin smile, "You, my friend is going to Florida."

Langichatte froze mid-chew. "Florida? You mean… Cold America? Captain, please, I'm sorry for anything you think I've done. Including that one time I dated your daughter."

"What, you dated my daughter?" the captain said.

Langichatte's mouth fell open. "Who told you that nasty rumor about me? Captain, please focus, don't send me to the land of fake paradise."

"It's already set… God knows I needed a break from you. You're flying out tomorrow."

Langichatte stood. "Captain, please, be reasonable. The last time I was in a room with air conditioning, I almost filed a lawsuit."

"Don't worry. The Americans requested you personally."

Langichatte look dumfounded. "They know me?"

The captain smiled wider. "Oh yes. You're famous now. International. That chase with the chicken thief? Already gone viral."

Langichatte looked down at the chicken bucket. "Was it the belt?"

"You're selling yourself short. It was more than just your belt. It's also your charm my friend. Your Jour de vie, I can tell you with definitive a surety, every time, I come to this precinct, I think of you. I enjoy reading the piles and piles of paperwork that sits on my desk almost every single day, about you. Nothing pleases me more, than spending my days, and days, and days… and days, reading reports about you. No, my friend, you're the type of person that can't, no longer stay local. You need to be, international. You will not deprive the world of your heroics. Your legend, needs a bigger stage."

Langichatte sighed dramatically, slung his sunglasses back on, and walked toward the exit. "If I freeze to death in America, make sure my casket is heated."

"Nonsense, a super hero like you can never die. Don't forget your belt," the captain called.

Langichatte waved it in the air. "Never leave home without it."

The crowd watched him go, some confused, others still holding claims for damages. Behind him, Chicken Thief Delly tried to sneak a piece of chicken. Langichatte turned back suddenly.

"Touch that, and I'll make you taste leather again."

Chicken Thief Delly froze.

Langichatte smiled and stepped out into the sun.

"Florida, here I come."

CHAPTER 2
BRIEFING IN THE STATES

Port-au-Prince International Airport 5:43 AM

The sun hadn't yet fully cracked the edge of the Haitian horizon, but Port-au-Prince International Airport was already buzzing with a chaotic kind of rhythm only morning travel could produce. Rolling luggage wheels clicked across the scuffed and cracked tiles like a thousand tiny metronomes, keeping time with the rising hum of travelers jockeying for position. Flip-flops slapped like impatient tambourines against the floor, punctuated by the occasional frustrated stomp from someone realizing they'd forgotten their passport… or worse, their charger.

In one corner, a baby wailed as though auditioning for an opera, her tiny lungs outmatching the nearby crowd. Her mother bounced and hushed, half singing, half pleading, sweat already glistening on her brow. A man in a bright floral shirt haggled with a vendor over a carved wooden drum he absolutely didn't need but couldn't walk away from. The vendor, practiced and persuasive, pointed out its "authentic spiritual resonance" while waving away mosquitoes with a rolled-up newspaper.

Overhead, a loudspeaker crackled to life, sputtering through a haze of static. A heavily accented voice attempted English, mangling flight numbers and destinations into a garbled stew of consonants and confusion. Heads tilted, eyebrows lifted, and then like a wave of resignation the crowd moved anyway, as if guided by intuition or divine travel instinct.

Amid it all, the scent of fried akra and strong coffee wafted through the terminal, grounding the madness in a familiar comfort.

This wasn't just a departure point it was a portal where chaos and excitement danced arm-in-arm, welcoming some home and sending others toward the unknown.

But none of it mattered to Langichatte LaBond.

He entered the terminal like a celebrity grand marshal stepping onto a carnival float slow, confident, magnetic. Heads turned not because they recognized him, but because they should. He moved with the casual authority of someone who had once dated a pop star, punched a crocodile, and survived a shootout in a karaoke bar all before lunch. His walk wasn't just a walk it was a vibe, a silent symphony that whispered, "Behold."

Green three-quarter length pants fluttered with every measured step, pressed to perfection despite the humidity's best efforts. His floral shirt, button all the way up like one of my top three favorite Fat Joe songs. His tie perfectly nodded backwards, defiantly hints to the world, this man is pure mystery and mischief. A pink suit jacket, he personally picks to wear to show his sensitivity side.

His sports white sox inside his dress church shoes. somehow both casual and authoritative, slapped against the floor in a rhythm that echoed his swagger: slow, intentional, poetic. And then there was the duffel oddly shaped, round at the base, and emitting a gentle steam as if it contained not clothes, but perhaps a freshly roasted goat or a very patient volcano. No one dared ask. One glance at the duffel and most folks instinctively stepped aside, the way pigeons' part for incoming taxis.

Langichatte's eyes scanned the terminal, not searching, just observing like a lion checking his domain for unnecessary movement. Every person in his path either stiffened or smiled, unsure whether to fear him, follow him, or ask for a selfie.

He approached the airline counter like it was a red carpet, and he was both the guest of honor and the event itself. With a flourish that might've seemed exaggerated on anyone else but felt perfectly natural on him Langichatte pulled out a laminated ID from his shirt pocket. It was slightly bent; the edges frayed like it had been through one too many laundromat adventures or last-minute arrests. He held it up with a proud grin:

The woman at the desk squinted at it. Her job had introduced her to all manner of characters armed diplomats, weeping evangelists, dreadlocked reggae legends, and one man who claimed to be the reincarnation of Toussaint Louverture. But this?

This was new.

Langichatte's badge wasn't just a document; it was a prop in a one-man show titled Swagger: The Musical. He displayed it like it was both a golden ticket and an engagement ring something you flash when you know the universe owes you a little favor.

The airline attendant didn't argue. She raised an eyebrow with the precision of someone who's seen everything and chooses not to react to any of it. Still, she slid the boarding passes across the counter with a faint smirk, half amused, half impressed.

Langichatte leaned in just enough to make her day interesting. (to no one in particular):

"First time leaving Haiti, and I don't even have to wait in line? Sweet life, baby."

As if summoned by his voice, the crowd behind him parted. Not in irritation or confusion, but reverence. It wasn't just a queue anymore it was a pathway, cleared by the sheer magnetism of a man who treated airport protocol like background music to his legend.

A young mother nearby clutched her daughter, trying to keep the child from wandering. But the toddler, eyes wide and curious, wriggled free for a moment. She looked at Langichatte with the kind of awe normally reserved for superheroes and cartoon princesses. Then, with tiny fingers curled in grace, she blew him a kiss.

Langichatte didn't miss a beat. He reached out and caught the invisible kiss mid-air, his movements tender and theatrical. Pressing it gently to his heart, he bowed his head as if receiving a royal blessing.

"Blessings to you, little princess," he said softly.

Then he stood tall again, gave the child a wink that could disarm a firing squad, and continued his royal promenade toward the security gate his duffel swinging, his Church shoes clacking on the cement floor, and the story of his legend already being whispered behind him.

At the TSA checkpoint, the carnival came to a screeching halt. As a TSA Agent Supervisor, a heavyset tall man and his two apprentices are working line C.

Langichatte strolled up to the security line with the same rhythm in his step that had carried him through the terminal still whistling a breezy kompa tune, still glowing with effortless confidence. But this was no longer his stage. This was America's stage, and its performers wore blue uniforms, black gloves, and expressions carved from concrete.

The conveyor belt stretched out before him like a challenge. Gray trays. Cold metal. Unblinking cameras. The smell of latex and unresolved tension. Around him, travelers fidgeted, undressing with quiet resentment. An old man wrestled with his belt. A teenager argued about a bottle of coconut oil. A baby screamed in protest as if it already sensed the violation of its future liberties.

Langichatte stopped, cocked his head, and surveyed the setup like a seasoned general eyeing enemy terrain. He glanced at the towering body scanner, the kind that made even innocent people feel guilty, and then at the three TSA agents flanking the gate as the supervisor looking like the before, whom was split into two after. Buzz-cuts, with the glares and weariness of people working sixteen-hour shifts. Under the watchful eyes of their TSA supervisor, apprentice #1 spoke "Sir, please step back sir. We can only check one person at a time."

Langichatte (with a diplomat's nod and a tourist's grin):

"Morning, officers."

He lifted his sunglasses with theatrical flair, revealing eyes that sparkled with charm and chaos. Then, with a flick of his wrist, he produced his Haitian passport like a magician pulling his final ace from a sleeve.

The TSA apprentice #1 didn't flinch, just like his supervisor taught him. He didn't even glance at the document.

(monotone, eyes on the screen):

"Shoes off. Belt off. Empty your pockets. Step into the scanner."

Langichatte glanced down at his footwear. Only he knew what his church shoes embarrassing secret was. (raising an eyebrow):

"My brother, my socks are moonroof. If I take these off, that's just skin and floor. You want that responsibility on your soul?"

Confused by his statement, both apprentices cracked a tiny smile but coughed it away behind their gloves.

TSA Agent Supervisor stone-faced took over:

"Still gotta scan you, sir."

Langichatte sighed with exaggerated pain. He bent down and peeled his shoes off slowly, as if removing a relic from sacred ground. And that's when the TSA agents understood what he was trying to say. They tried not to laugh. But someone in the line screamed out "Wow my brother. What foreign land did you go to, to buy those Swiss cheese socks from."

Everyone laughs.

Langichatte (Loudly responded):

"Ask your mother, she sold them to me."

Again, everyone laughs. Langichatte turns back to the TSA agents

"The floor is cold. I have droptop, convertible socks on, please, let me put my shoes back on."

He dropped his belt, a half-eaten mango wrapped in wax paper, a wooden prayer bead necklace, and two loose batteries.

The agent eyed the items like he was trying to decide whether to laugh or call Homeland Security.

Langichatte stepped into the scanner, arms raised like he was surrendering to the absurdity of modern travel. The machine buzzed and whirred. (murmuring):

"If this thing detects ancestral spirits, I'm suing."

Langichatte didn't just stand still he posed. One hand on his hip, one eyebrow raised, the curve of a smirk playing on his lips. (to the scanner):

"Make sure you get my good side. That's the left. The right's for my enemies."

Moments later, the machine beeped. One agent motioned him aside for a pat-down.

apprentice #2 (trying to sound official):

"Sir, the scanner's picking up an anomaly on your lower back. Please remain still."

Langichatte blinked, then broke into a grin.

"That's not an anomaly, my friend. That's just charisma."

The two apprentice again chuckled despite themselves and apprentice #1 gave him a light pat-down. No weapons. No contraband. Just heat, swagger, and an unreasonable amount of body oil.

The TSA apprentice #2 young, thin, clearly new reached for Langichatte's duffel bag. His latex gloves squeaked slightly as he unzipped the top flap. He leaned in. Then he froze.

The scent hit him like a Creole gospel choir busting through a cathedral door on Resurrection Sunday.

Smoked chicken in onion sauce. Pikliz sharp enough to baptize your nose. Spiced black bean puree that told stories of grandmothers and resistance. Cilantro white rice so fragrant it felt illegal in three states. The divine Mamma Lovelie made this food at 20% discount in the famous Kokoye Restaurant in Pétion Ville. Just so, her number one customer would have something to eat on the plane.

The line behind Langichatte halted. Time slowed. Phones came out. Eyebrows lifted. A baby, mid-tantrum, suddenly went quiet. Even the floor seemed to hum reverently.

Immediately The TSA supervisor knew he had to take control of the situation, eyes wide. (sniffing, stunned):

"Sir... what is this?"

Langichatte approached like a loving uncle explaining Christmas to a child. (beaming):

"Breakfast. Lunch. And a little something I call the pre-dinner warm-up. All prepared by the hands of the divine Mamma Lovelie chef, healer, sorceress of spice."

He kissed two fingers and pointed toward the ceiling.

TSA Supervisor:

"You can't bring this much food on the plane, sir."

Langichatte laughed a rich, rolling belly laugh that echoed like a drumline.

"Of course I can! Look sealed. No leaks. No drama. Just passion and protein, my friend."

TSA Supervisor (growing firm):

"No outside food past security. Especially... this much. You'll have to throw it away or we'll throw it away for you."

Langichatte recoiled like the man had just slapped his mother.

(gasping):

"Throw away Haitian food? In this economy? Are you possessed?"

TSA Supervisor (robotic):

"There will be food on the plane, sir."

Langichatte's face twisted slowly from offense to disbelief.

(arms crossed):

"Will it be Haitian food?"

TSA Supervisor (snorting, then catching himself):

"No, sir. It'll be more... fancy."

Langichatte stepped forward, eyes like twin embers now.

(dangerously calm):

"More fancy than diri blan, poul avek sauce and pua nwa? My brother... You disrespect every grandmother who ever danced in front of a hot stove."

People behind him began murmuring in agreement.

"Man got a point..."

"That's sacred food..."

"I'd fight over pikliz too."

The TSA Supervisor had no hesitation to give for his actions. His grip on the bag wasn't loosening. Apprentice #2 leaned in with a whisper.

"Dude, this smells amazing. Maybe we shouldn't discard it. And keep it for our lunch today." But the supervisor gave him a look, like a parent to a child- stay in your place.

Langichatte turned slightly toward the crowd, lifting one metal bowl like Simba over Pride Rock.

"You see this? This isn't food. This is a national archive. A spice memoir. A love letter from Mamma Lovelie to the entire diaspora. I'm not going on no flights without my Haitian food. I didn't even wanted to go anyway. Tu a crazy, if tu penser je monter de plane sans mou manje."

The TSA Supervisor took back the metal bowl from Langichatte's hands. Visibly with an attitude. "Well, you're going to get your wish today because we will not allow you to get on this plane with all this food. And that's final." Just then, his phone rang.

"Checkpoint Three who the hell is calling me right now. I'm busy dealing with one of those backwater Haitians. Oh, I'm so sorry sir. I didn't know it was you sir. But. But. But. It's three metal bowls sir. All three metal bowls sir? But sir! Are you sure that's wise sir? I didn't know your wife is Haitian sir. No, your wife is a lovely lady sir. I understand"

He hung up slowly. His entire body language changed. He stood straighter. Paler. More respectful (to his apprentices):

"He's cleared to board. With all the food. Apprentice #1 you are now the new supervisor." Then turn to Langichatte "I promise you, I will repay you for your kindness today." As he threw his badge in the garbage and walk off.

Oblivious, Langichatte placed the bowls back in the bag with the tenderness of a surgeon replacing a heart. He turned to TSA Apprentice #2 with a slow smile.

(smirking):

"I'll take my bag now, thank you. Oh, and what's this? You were hoping to snag a bite on your lunch break? Sorry to disappoint, boss."

He zipped the bag with deliberate, exaggerated flair and slung it over his shoulder.

As he walked toward the gate, every footstep echoed like a victory drum. People cheered quietly. One woman wiped a tear. A small child held up a drawing of Langichatte riding a flying mango. Someone yelled, "Long live Mamma Lovelie from Kokoye!"

Langichatte waved once, kissed the air, and whispered:

"And that, my friends, is how you season security."

Boarding the plane was surprisingly uneventful but only because nobody dared challenge the man who had just secured a presidential override for three steaming bowls

of Haitian food. The passengers and crew alike felt the gravity of Langichatte's presence, like a king entering his domain, and quietly stepped aside.

Langichatte sauntered down the aisle with a confidence that made the designer luggage and business suits part like the Red Sea. He settled into his first-class leather seat with a regal ease, as if the plush cushions carried the weight of his ancestors' blessings. With deliberate care, he placed his round-bottomed duffel bag on the floor and began unpacking his treasure: the three metal bowls, each wrapped carefully in a cloth that smelled of home.

Flight attendants appeared, gliding over with menus offering citrus-glazed halibut, asparagus soufflé, and a dizzying array of gourmet dishes that might as well have been alien cuisine. Langichatte's laughter was soft, almost a chuckle of gentle amusement.

"You people don't even know what food is," he said, shaking his head.

First, he unscrewed the lid of Bowl #1, revealing fluffy cilantro-lime white rice flecked with aromatic thyme and cloves. Then, Bowl #2 opened to crispy, golden chicken thighs simmered in epazote and a fiery habanero sauce dress in Haitian pikliz that seemed to radiate warmth. Last was Bowl #3, a thick, velvety black bean sauce, rich enough to resurrect a person from heartbreak.

As he began to savor the meal, the intoxicating scent filled the first-class cabin, drifting into the noses of fellow passengers. The man sitting next to Langichatte grimaced and gagged, trying to hide his disgust behind a tight-lipped frown.

"Some of us paid for gourmet food," the passenger sneered, voice dripping with snobbery.

Without even looking up, Langichatte replied with a sly grin,

"And some of us brought it."

Across the aisle, a young influencer, who could have been Jessie Woo whipped out her phone and began quietly recording. "Y'all... look at this man," she whispered to her audience, voice hushed but full of disbelief. "Home-cooked buffet in first class. Third-world flex gone wrong."

Langichatte caught her eye and leaned toward her phone, delivering his lines with the calm confidence of a seasoned actor.

"Bonjour, world. Let the record show: you eat for style. I eat for flavor. We are not the same."

The video went viral, exploding to over 24.3 million views under hashtags like #ChickenKing, #LangichatteEats, and #ThisIsNotCoach.

By the time dessert was served, even the snide passenger had slid a plastic spoon toward Langichatte, sheepishly asking for a taste. Langichatte handed him a small sample with a gracious smile.

"Next time," he said warmly, "bring a fork and humility."

The cabin settled into a quiet reverence. Full bellies, stunned glances, and Langichatte sitting back with three empty bowls, a clean conscience, and the unmistakable look of a man ready to shake up the American government.

Secret Government Installation, Everglades, Florida

_11:03 AM_

By the time Langichatte's flight descended over Florida, the skies had cleared into an endless canvas of blinding blue, the sun casting harsh, unfiltered light across the sprawling Everglades below. From the window seat, the thick swaths of marsh grass and winding waterways looked like veins pulsing life beneath a fragile crust of civilization. But inside the plane, a different kind of pulse was quickening electric, expectant, charged with the kind of curiosity that only viral fame can generate.

Across the cabin, whispers floated like secrets on the stale recycled air. His infamous moment the image of a man eating three bowls of Haitian food in the lap of American luxury had spread faster than wildfire on social media. Passengers and crew alike were caught in the ripple effect.

Flight attendants exchanged knowing glances behind the galley curtain, their voices hushed but tinged with excitement.

"He's famous now," one said, voice low, "he eats like my abuela."

Langichatte lay back in his seat, eyes closed behind dark sunglasses, savoring the moment. He was aware of the quiet buzz, but it didn't bother him. He had bigger things to think about than the fleeting chatter of passengers. The weight of what lay ahead pressed down on him far more than the judgment or fascination of a few strangers.

When the plane touched down on the sunbaked tarmac of a private airfield deep in the Everglades, the mood shifted sharply. The moment his feet touched the polished concrete of the jet bridge, the casual amusement evaporated, replaced by a cold, unyielding seriousness that wrapped around him like a steel cage.

Waiting at the bottom of the private stairway were three black SUVs sleek, formidable, lined up like chess pieces in a high-stakes game. Their glossy exteriors reflected the harsh sunlight, while tinted windows obscured the faces inside.

Five agents stood beside the vehicles, each dressed head to toe in matching black suits and earpieces that hummed with quiet communication. Their posture was rigid, almost unnatural, as if carved from granite rather than flesh and bone. Their eyes, cold and unblinking, tracked Langichatte's every movement, calculating and unreadable.

The tallest among them stepped forward, a man whose square jaw seemed permanently clenched and whose facial warmth could be measured only in degrees above zero. He removed his sunglasses to reveal eyes steely and unreadable.

"Langichatte LaBond?" he asked flatly, voice clipped and professional.

Langichatte lifted a hand, fingers spread wide in a mock wave a game show host acknowledging the winner.

"In the flesh," he replied with a grin, "though a bit colder than usual."

He pulled his duffel bag tighter against his side, shivering slightly despite the heat. The transition from Haiti's tropical embrace to this sanitized, government-controlled air felt like a cruel joke a sudden switch from sun-drenched freedom to a sterile, suffocating cold that gnawed at his skin.

Agent Rogers his name was pinned neatly to the lapel of his suit was already turning toward one of the SUVs.

"You'll come with us," Rogers said, voice still flat.

Langichatte followed without protest, stepping into the back of the vehicle, which was luxuriously appointed with black leather seats that contrasted sharply with the tense atmosphere. The ride was silent except for the faint hum of the air conditioning set to a level that might freeze a penguin mid-waddle.

He rubbed his arms, trying to warm the chill that had settled deep in his bones.

"Why are Americans so allergic to room temperature?" he muttered under his breath. "This feels like I'm being punished for having pores."

The convoy rolled out onto winding roads flanked by towering palm trees that cast long, flickering shadows over the cracked asphalt. Gradually, the lush greenery gave way to dense swampland, where mangroves clawed at the sky and waterlogged earth squelched beneath the tires.

At one point, the SUVs passed a weathered sign, cartoonish in its irreverence: a grinning alligator wearing dark sunglasses, accompanied by the text "Last chance to turn around."

Langichatte smirked, raising an eyebrow. "You sure this is the turn-around, or the entrance to Narnia?"

The scenery shifted abruptly. The paved roads gave way to fortified concrete barriers, watchtowers looming like silent sentinels against the cloudless sky. A camouflaged checkpoint awaited, guarded by soldiers with rifles slung over their shoulders and faces hardened into masks of discipline and suspicion.

A massive sliding gate groaned open slowly, a steel leviathan hissing like a beast exhaling after a long sleep.

Beyond lay the secret facility an imposing structure built to intimidate. The architecture was brutalist, a fortress of gray concrete slabs, razor wire, electrified fencing, and guard towers bristling with weaponry. Surveillance drones buzzed overhead like mechanical hawks, their lenses trained on every movement, every breath.

Langichatte's gaze flicked to the perimeter, then to a bizarre sight near the fence: two German shepherds, sporting military vest emblazoned with what looked suspiciously like two different serial numbers. They bowed their head and saluted as the SUV passed.

Langichatte whispered, almost amused: "You people put animals on payroll, too? No wonder your budget's a mess."

The SUVs came to a halt in front of a set of steel doors embedded into the earth, camouflaged so perfectly that they might have been part of the swamp itself. These were the gates to Facility Echo-9, the mysterious hive where Langichatte would spend the coming weeks preparing for the mission ahead.

Agent Rogers's voice was monotone as the doors groaned open. "This is Facility Echo-9. You'll be debriefed, processed, and assigned quarters for the duration of your training."

Langichatte mocked a salute. "Training? I thought I was here to bust a drug lord, not audition for a space station."

Rogers replied flatly, "You're not a 00-agent number yet."

The cold inside hit Langichatte like a physical blow. The temperature was merciless an arctic chill designed to smother any lingering warmth or joy. He shivered violently, clutching at his shirt collar as if it might hold back the frostbite.

"Why is it freezing in here?" he demanded. "What, y'all store dead bodies in the vents?"

No one answered.

"I'm serious," he said louder. "This feels like refrigerator air designed by Satan's accountant."

Agent Rogers responded, deadpan: "We keep the internal temperature at 61°F. It improves alertness."

Langichatte shot back immediately, "You know what else improves alertness? Being alive. I'm alert right now. Alert that my nose and ears are dying."

A young agent nearby struggled to keep from laughing. Rogers gave him a look that could erase pensions and break wills.

They walked past rows of high-security doors marked with ominous labels: "Containment," "Weapons R&D," "Zero-Gravity Test Bay," and "Psych Eval – Agent Use Only."

Langichatte peered through a window on one door and saw a man floating in mid-air, clutching what looked like a grenade and a guitar.

"What kind of X-Files Disneyland is this?" he whispered.

Processing Langichatte

Langichatte was led to a biometric chamber, where a robotic voice methodically scanned his retina, fingerprints, and attempted to take a hair sample only to fail repeatedly because of the thick cocoa butter he liberally applied to protect his skin. The robotic arm slipped and recoiled as if it had touched something too slippery for science.

They issued him a badge with a label that read:

"Temporary Status – Probationary Field Observer (International Mole Class)"

Langichatte stared at it, incredulous.

"You made me sound like a half-spy, half-vermin," he said. "What is this? A raccoon internship?"

The tech handing over the badge avoided eye contact.

"Temporary… until you pass clearance," he muttered.

Langichatte smiled thinly. "Oh, I'll pass. Just make sure the heater in my room works. And if not, I'll sleep next to the missile core. I'm sure it's warm."

The Dorm Room

They finally showed him his quarters a small, metal-paneled room, bare except for a narrow bed that looked like it belonged in a jail cell, topped with a blanket so thin it might've been stolen from a dollhouse.

There was one window, a tiny, barred aperture that looked directly into a dimly lit hallway, like a prison cell's last mockery of freedom. Even 100 feet underground the designed architect still felt windows were necessary.

Langichatte stood in the center of the room and spoke to the ceiling, assuming his room was bugged with listening devices. His voice carrying the kind of sarcastic desperation only a man out of place can summon.

"Okay, government people," he said. "I need to file a formal request: One. Warm blanket. Two. Heater. Three. Plantain chips. Four. An AC technician to explain why the devil has a thermostat in this building in the middle of January in Florida."

Silence. No reply. Disappointment was written all over his face.

He pulled out his bowls, unstacked them, and arranged them carefully on the metal desk as if laying out spiritual relics.

"Stay strong, my loves," he whispered. "This cold cannot touch your flavor."

Echo-9 Briefing Hall, Government Facility

1:17 PM

Langichatte entered the briefing room the same way he entered everywhere else with the posture of a man who believed the world was one long red carpet rolled out just for him. His confident stride echoed softly against the polished floors, a stark contrast to the sterile seriousness surrounding him. The room was sleek and shockingly clean almost unnaturally so. It smelled like disinfectant, fear, and printer ink, a strange blend that made the air feel heavier than it should.

Holographic displays flickered to life along the walls as digital projectors buzzed softly overhead. A long, black-glass conference table stretched toward a massive screen, flanked by serious-looking people in suits who blinked very little and smiled even less. Their

eyes were sharp, scanning, filled with unspoken tension and years of experience hidden beneath their calm exteriors.

Langichatte slid into the last seat at the table, a full twenty minutes late and with a coconut-flavored protein bar sticking out of his back pocket like a badge of casual defiance. He barely noticed the stares he was used to being the odd one out, and honestly, he didn't care.

He took a quick scan of the room:

Three tactical specialists, all with tight haircuts and tighter jaws, looking like they meant business with or without weapons.

Two CIA representatives, both scribbling into leather-bound notebooks like court reporters at a high-stakes spy trial, their pens moving in sync with the weight of every word spoken.

And at the front, presiding over the meeting like a grim high school principal, stood Agent Gil Arenas.

Arenas wore the same scowl as before, but this time, it feels more justifiable. ZoGod killed one of his agents. So, payback must come soon in agent Arenas' mindset. His piercing eyes glowed faintly beneath the sharp light, and he tapped a glowing tablet that suddenly burst to life in front of him.

A 3D holographic projection floated midair a lifelike image of the infamous Haitian drug lord, ZoGod. The figure rotated slowly, showing a man dressed in an unbuttoned silk shirt, gold chains glinting, and sunglasses with mirrored lenses that somehow reflected your shame back at you.

Agent Arenas' voice cut through the silence:

"This is the man we're after."

Everyone leaned in, the tension thickening like humidity before a storm.

Langichatte leaned back, crossing one leg over the other with the calm of a man who didn't need to prove anything yet. He raised a hand with a sly grin.

"Before we begin, where's the part of the briefing where they offer me gloves and a jacket? Because I'm pretty sure I just caught pneumonia from breathing in this refrigerator you call a meeting room."

The agents ignored him, except for one Agent Carmichael, seated two chairs down. She had tactical braids, sharp cheekbones, and an aura that whispered, "Don't test me."

Agent Carmichael:

"Mr. LaBond, please pay attention."

Langichatte gave a mock salute, his smile wide but respectful:

"Yes, ma'am. Cold and cranky. Noted."

Arenas swiped across the tablet, and ZoGod's hologram zoomed out to reveal a sprawling digital map of drug trafficking routes arteries of red and blue lines stretching from the coast of Florida down into the Caribbean, spiderwebbing across Haiti-like veins filled with poison.

Agent Arenas explained:

"Jean-Paul Joseph alias ZoGod controls the third-largest narco-empire in the Western Hemisphere. He operates front businesses, encrypted social media channels, crypto casinos, and mobile weaponized fleets. But we need hard evidence to prove all of this. Every time we close in, he vanishes. Five failed attempts to capture him. Four are on record."

Langichatte's voice cut through, curious and sharp:

"What happened to the fifth one?"

The room hesitated. Agent Arenas paused, then Agent Carmichael answered dryly:

"We don't talk about the submarine incident."

Langichatte raised his eyebrows, impressed:

"Submarine? That's a man with ambition."

Arenas nodded, tapping on a holographic file that exploded into a slow-motion video.

The footage showed ZoGod walking off a flaming boat, adjusting his velvet robe, and sipping a drink from a coconut while a tiger followed him off the wreckage. Behind them, a stunned SWAT team scrambled.

Langichatte chuckled, genuinely impressed:

"Okay, but why does the tiger always look so relaxed?"

A few agents chuckled softly. Arenas cleared his throat, regaining control of the room.

"We've traced his current operations to a growing network in Florida. He's using Miami as a base to traffic drugs directly into Haiti. The situation has escalated."

He tapped again. The conference table glowed with crime scene photos, arrest logs, marked territory maps, and blurry surveillance stills showing briefcases being exchanged in nightclubs, swamps, and even an outdoor yoga class.

Agent Carmichael spoke with a sharp edge:

"If this pipeline is completed, it will flood both Miami and Haiti with high-potency narcotics. Overdoses have increased by 23% in the last three months. The DEA, CIA, and our Bureau are all on high alert."

Langichatte's face darkened as he leaned forward, his voice low and steady:

"He's poisoning my people."

Agent Carmichael nodded solemnly:

"Yes. But Haiti is just the beginning. The man is targeting the hole Caribbean islands."

A brief silence fell over the room, thick with the weight of the mission ahead. Then Langichatte sat back and smiled widely, a spark of fire returning to his eyes.

"Then I guess we're going tiger owner hunting."

Suddenly, an intern in a tight gray polo approached with a sleek black suitcase, hands trembling slightly.

Intern (nervously):

"Sir, these are your issued tools, as discussed. Prototype gear non-lethal by default. Highly sensitive. Be careful."

Langichatte popped open the case. Inside, nestled in velvet compartments, lay:

A tiny listening device, delicate but powerful

A non-lethal silver pistol, sleek and unassuming

A set of digital lock picks, gleaming with potential

What looked like a fancy inhaler, mysterious and high-tech

And a black spherical object with a soft blue light pulsing at its core

Langichatte picked up the sphere, grinning:

"What's this? A Bluetooth speaker?"

Agent Carmichael snapped, alarmed:

"Don't !"

Click.

The sphere blinked twice. Then everything went dark.

WHUMMMMP.

An invisible pulse rippled through the room, followed by the hiss of dying electronics. The holograms fizzled out. The wall displays went black. The fluorescent lights above popped like angry popcorn. A nearby coffee machine exploded, shooting scalding foam into the air.

Langichatte blinked in the sudden silence, smoke curling around him:

"…My bad. I thought it was a Bluetooth speaker."

Agent Carmichael stared at her dead tablet, grim:

"That was a Class-2 localized EMP grenade."

Langichatte waved the smoke from his face with a grin:

"You know, back in Haiti, we call that pressing the wrong button. It's very common. National sport."

Agent Arenas, furious, growled:

"You just shorted out a million dollars of classified tech."

Langichatte shrugged, unapologetic:

"I hope you're not trying to blame me for your mistake. When you were buying those techs, they probably told you to upgrade to the 10-million-dollar techs, cause it protects against EMP's. But you decided to be cheap and buy the 1-million-dollar one. Look what happened, this is 100% your fault."

Agent Arenas stood upset and bewildered at the same time. "How did you know there was an upgrade?"

Langichatte (smiling):

"Ha Ha! My friend, in government, that's smoking mirror 101. In Haiti, we always buy the 10 years old computers for 200 US each to show the people we're fiscally conservative, but our budget never goes down. But let's get serious, I didn't come from Port-au-Prince just to freeze in your air-conditioned rooms and you admiring my mind. When can I get into the fight?"

CHAPTER 3
THE PLAN

FBI Training Facility Next Day – Everglades, Florida 6:04 AM

The sun was nowhere to be found no hint of its usual warm glow, not even a flicker behind thick, gray clouds. The early dawn mist hung low, draping the open-air training courtyard in a ghostly veil. A thin sheet of cold air clung stubbornly to the ground, as if frost's clumsy cousin had decided to crash Florida's famous warmth with an uninvited surprise visit.

Langichatte LaBond stood dead center in the courtyard, utterly still except for his bare knees, which twitched uncontrollably. They shook like two maracas caught in a salsa band, betraying the cold that even his best efforts couldn't shake. January in Florida is not always sunny.

He exhaled slowly, watching his breath curl in small, visible puffs that disappeared into the mist.

Langichatte (murmuring like a heartbroken lover):

"Why… am I seeing my breath every time I exhale? Sunny Florida. Where the brochure promised sweat, not suffering. They be lying, that's why they invented the fine print."

He tightened his floral shirt around himself a gesture more symbolic than practical. The shirt button up as always with a backward tie on his neck but still offered no warmth; it might as well have been a postcard fluttering in the chill wind. His linen three-quarter pants flapped limply like faded flags at half-mast. On his feet, his mismatched wool socks one pink, one orange, both pilfered from the lost and found made him look like a bewildered tourist trapped in a punishment-themed resort.

and dress shoes clacked against frost-kissed tiles, their mournful sound echoing his discomfort. Langichatte was glaringly out of place.

Around him, the other recruits were everything he wasn't: tough, toned, and tactical. They stretched in sleek black thermals and heavy combat boots, some jogging laps with focused intensity, others pounding out push-ups on gravel. Meanwhile, Langichatte hugged himself, shivering, like he was rehearsing for a one-man reenactment of Titanic.

Langichatte (squinting at the gray sky):

"Florida, they said. Sunshine State, they said. All lies. They should rename this place the Frostbite Peninsula. Or better yet, sell it back to nature and apologize."

His teeth began to chatter loudly. He stomped in place, desperate to get circulation back into his numb ankles.

Two agents jogged past, exchanging a quick, muttered comment that sounded like, "What the hell is he wearing?" Langichatte didn't respond; he was conserving energy. He'd already decided that, mid-shiver, he'd only speak when necessary or when sarcasm might keep him alive.

Suddenly, a voice cut through the cold morning air like a sniper's bullet.

Agent Carmichael (approaching briskly):

"Mr. LaBond, it's 64 degrees."

Langichatte didn't flinch. He slowly turned, his entire expression a theatrical mix of heartbreak and disbelief.

(voice trembling, tone dramatically defeated):

"That's not a temperature. That's a threat."

Without missing a beat, Carmichael passed him, unfazed, tossing a comment over her shoulder like a bone to a freezing dog.

"Welcome to America."

Langichatte shouted after her, the last vestige of defiance cracking his voice:

"You people need Jesus and a heater!"

She kept walking.

Langichatte shuffled over to the nearest bench and sat down like a man trying not to freeze to cold metal.

From his back pocket, he pulled a crumpled emergency blanket a shiny foil sheet he'd "borrowed" from the infirmary and wrapped it tightly around his shoulders.

He blew warm breath into his cupped hands, willing the cold to retreat, when he noticed a small squirrel perched atop the fence, watching him intently.

The squirrel blinked.

Langichatte blinked back.

(grinning despite himself):

"You think this is funny, huh? Little ice demon."

The squirrel flicked its tail and scampered away, as if laughing at his misery.

Langichatte sat in silence for a moment before pulling a thermos from his bag. He unscrewed the lid, hoping for warmth. Instead, steam was absent, and the liquid inside a lukewarm hibiscus tea tasted like betrayal.

(grimacing as he took a sip):

"Even my tea gave up."

Then, a buzzer sounded sharply over the loudspeaker.

Disembodied Voice:

"Training cycle begins in ten minutes. All recruits report to Formation Point Bravo. Appropriate dress code required."

Langichatte stood slowly, still wrapped in his foil blanket and mismatched socks.

(to no one in particular):

"I swear, if I survive this place, I'm retiring somewhere with real sun. Maybe near a volcano."

He trudged toward the formation area, trailing a foil cape and defiance behind him like a shivering prophet marching toward battle. Agent Carmichael run after him

"Hey LaBond, disregard that last message from the blowhorn. You need to report to agent Arenas right away"

Briefing Annex, Echo-9 Facility – Everglades, Florida

7:13 AM

The atmosphere was thick with the scent of electronics, cables, and the unmistakable tension of high stakes the kind of pressure that made you hold your breath without realizing it. The briefing annex room all most look the same as yesterday's meeting room. But the equipment here definitely looks EMP protected.

Dominating the center of the room was a large, round black-glass table, sleek and polished to a mirror shine. Embedded monitors lined its edges, pulsing gently with a soft blue light, like a sleeping beast waiting to be awakened. Around this table sat a small group: two analysts deeply engrossed in their data streams, fingers flying over keyboards; a cyber-intelligence liaison typing furiously, eyes sharp and alert; Agent Carmichael, ever composed with tactical braids pulled tight, her gaze steady and unyielding; and finally, Langichatte LaBond.

Langichatte was wrapped in his crumpled emergency blanket, the shiny foil a stark contrast against the high-tech surroundings. He rocked slowly in his chair, shoulders hunched, as if the cold hadn't yet loosened its grip on him. His eyes stared blankly at the holographic projections, but his mind was somewhere else maybe replaying the frostbitten morning or weighing the long list of life choices that had landed him in this room. The quiet hum of technology surrounded him, but for now, Langichatte was a cold man lost in thought, waiting for the briefing to begin.

Langichatte pulled the emergency blanket tighter around his shoulders, the thin foil doing little to stave off the chill that had settled deep in his bones. He looked down at it with a mixture of gratitude and irony, speaking softly as if to an old friend.

(to his blanket):

"You are the only warmth I have in this world now. May our bond never be broken."

The foil crinkled faintly as he shifted, the sound oddly comforting in the otherwise silent room.

At the far end of the table stood Agent Gil Arenas his posture rigid, every inch the embodiment of discipline and control. His expression was carved from stone, a mask of unwavering focus that seemed to absorb the room's tension like a black hole. "LaBond, this is your second and last briefing until you pass your test. This is a very dangerous mission, so we want to make sure you know exactly what you're getting yourself into."

Langichatte's gaze flicked from the blanket to the map, the weight of the mission pressing down on him heavier than the cold ever could. This was no longer just about

surviving the frostbite or the bureaucracy it was about dismantling a web that stretched through Miami's underworld and beyond, and he was now part of that fight.

Langichatte leaned forward, the chill forgotten as his eyes locked onto the glowing display. He scanned every detail with sharp focus, the digital map revealing layers beneath layers of ZoGod's empire.

There were drug labs hidden deep in the industrial maze of Hialeah facilities camouflaged as ordinary warehouses but humming with illegal activity. Shipping depots by day, toxic hubs by night. Front businesses that masked operations so well they blurred the line between legitimate and criminal.

His gaze shifted to the neon-lit nightlife districts, where underground crypto casinos thrived behind velvet ropes and flashing signs. These clubs accepted only digital currency or pure gold an elite playground where paper trails evaporated and secrets were traded in whispers and encrypted code.

This was no simple cartel. It was a living, breathing organism, sprawling like a network of digital roots threading through Miami's concrete jungle complex, hidden, and dangerously alive.

Then, hovering just above the map, the air shimmered and ZoGod's face materialized in a 3D hologram. The image rotated slowly, capturing every angle with eerie realism. His grin was wide and confident, as if he held the key to secrets nobody else dared to uncover.

ZoGod was dressed like a king of decadence a white velvet robe trimmed in gold, oversized sunglasses reflecting flickering firelight, and a beard so perfectly groomed it looked like a crafted weapon. The sight made Langichatte mutter an unprintable phrase in Creole, a mix of disbelief, frustration, and grudging respect.

Agent Arenas' voice cut through the room like steel.

"Until you pass your qualifying tests, you have no field authority. No badge. No firearm clearance. We're planning to send you in the belly of the beast on a three-day mission. Your job is to woo this woman. Her name is Rose. And has far we can tell, she's not with the shenanigans, but she does have ZoGod ear and respect. So, we want to know what she knows. And remember, you are not a spy. You are a mole. Your job is to observe, report, and do nothing else. Understand?"

Langichatte stayed still for a moment, wrapped in his crinkling foil blanket, the only sound a faint rustle as he shifted. Then, slowly, he nodded once, deliberately.

"I observe. I report. I shiver. I got it."

The room was silent for a beat, the weight of the words hanging heavy in the cold air.

Then, almost sotto voice, Langichatte muttered, as if confessing a secret to the room's shadows:

"And if the coffee machine breaks again, I won't hold back my tears."

Agent Carmichael's lips curled into a subtle smirk, the corner of an analyst's mouth twitched with suppressed laughter. Arenas, as always, remained unreadable, his stone-cold gaze locked on the map before them.

Without breaking eye contact, Arenas pointed firmly to the glowing cityscape projected above the table.

"In two weeks, we launch Operation Ocean Lock a coordinated strike against ZoGod's Miami hub. Multi-agency, multi-national. Every resource, every drone, every satellite trained on him. We shut down the ports. We shut down his crypto transfers. We freeze his assets. This man has no limit, the street calls him the commander in chief, who knockout teeth. Plus, he killed one of our own. Our beloved, Agent Curtis, just a week after the man got promoted to the A -Unit. This man is a cold assassin, that needs to be ethered."

The map flickered and zoomed into a shipping yard near Biscayne Bay. Redacted files floated beside it codenames, blurred photos, surveillance timestamps.

Arenas continues:

"Look LaBond, this is not the type of criminals you used to deal with in Haiti. This man is a real-life bad guy. The worst of the worst. My higher-up's want to send you back home. They think we made a mistake, asking the Haitian government for help."

Langichatte slowly sat upright. His sarcasm dulled for a beat.

"Don't be like them coach. You pick the right superstar for your dream team. I'll bring home the gold."

Agent Carmichael:

"Pass the four test we're training you on. That will let us know if you're a starter or a bench player.'"

Langichatte exhaled sharply. He felt something churn in his stomach and it wasn't just the cold.

Agent Arenas (flat):

"We're giving you two weeks. Pass your tests, and you'll operate as Agent 009 with full authority. If you don't "

Langichatte (interrupting, smirking):

"I go back to Haiti with shame and frostbite?"

Arenas (coldly):

"Wrong. we'll send you to the gun fight anyway, with just your hands. And I promise you ZoGod will send you back to us in a box."

Silence fell over the room like a sudden snowfall.

Langichatte blinked. His mouth opened slightly, then closed. He stared at the map again. At the red dots. At the face of the man who dared to target his people. Then he slowly, wordlessly pulled the foil blanket tighter around his shoulders.

(softly, to himself):

"I better pass those damn tests."

Agent Carmichael (watching him):

"You've got heart, Langichatte. But heart won't get you through this. Training will. Discipline will. Focus will."

Langichatte turned to her, the blanket bunched under his chin like a child at story time.

(smiling faintly):

"I've got a bit of those. Somewhere in my luggage."

She didn't smile back, but she didn't look away.

Arenas (final words):

"Dismissed."

Langichatte stood slowly, stretched, and shuffled toward the door.

Then he stopped, turned, and looked one last time at ZoGod's face, rotating in ghostly silence.

"Your robe's nice, my friend. Let's see how it looks when I put you in handcuffs."

He left the room.

Echo-9 Training Compound

Day 1: Hand-to-Hand Combat – "The Human Pretzel"

The combat arena reeked of sweat, bruised egos, and hard-earned pride. The walls were plastered with punching bags, each one scarred from countless hits, and thick mats covered the floor, designed not just to soften falls but to catch shattered confidence. Cameras perched silently in the corners, humming quietly as they captured every move in

crisp 4K destined for "performance feedback" or, depending on the day's results, viral meme material.

Langichatte strode into the arena wearing a tank top boldly embla-zoned with the Haitian flag and shorts that looked like they'd been repur-posed from old beach curtains. His entrance was theatrical, carrying the swagger of a man who'd just stepped off a Caribbean dance floor.

Langichatte (grinning at a small group of watching trainees):

"This is where I shine. My body is a weapon. My fists are justice. My feet... are Caribbean poetry."

He spun with flourish, launching two playful air jabs that barely cut the space, then finished with a spinning heel kick that leaned more toward a pirouette than a strike. He wobbled on landing but caught himself with a theatrical bow.

A few smirks broke out among the trainees, one slow, appreciative clap echoing through the arena. Agent Carmichael raised an eyebrow, clearly unimpressed.

The combat instructor's voice cut in, dry and unamused:

"Your opponent: Agent Stone."

The heavy door at the far end hissed open, and a shadow stepped through. Felicia Stone was every bit the warrior: sculpted like a Greek statue forged for battle, tattoos snaking

down her arms like a war map, and hands sheathed in combat gloves that had ended more than a few fights.

Langichatte's grin faltered.

(muttering under his breath):

"Is there... maybe a friendlier Stone available? Perhaps one less forged in fire?"

The instructor nodded sharply.

"Begin."

DING!

Langichatte barely had time to blink.

When he opened his eyes again, Felicia had closed the gap effortlessly, dodging his hesitant jab like she was reading his every thought. Then, without warning, she swept his legs out from under him sending him crashing to the mat.

WHUMP!

The air whooshed from Langichatte's lungs. Before he could gather himself, Felicia flipped him again, sending him airborne before catching him mid-fall in a textbook arm bar. Without missing a beat, she twisted into a modified cobra lock, a move so old it hadn't been seen since World War II.

Langichatte howled into the mat.

(slapping the floor in defeat):

"I yield! I surrender! I believe in equality but not in martial arts therapy!"

Felicia released him with the gentleness of a kite string slipping free.

(standing over him, smirking):

"Sweetie, maybe try knitting. Or pottery. Something soft."

Langichatte rolled off the mat like over-kneaded dough slipping from a table.

(limping away, shaking his head):

"My ancestors watched that. They're lighting candles."

Day 2: Shooting Accuracy – "The Sniper of Sadness"

The shooting range was a cathedral of silence. Not the kind that comforted, but the one that weighed heavy in your chest, demanding concentration and respect. Rows of lanes stretched out like the ribs of some mechanical beast, each one marked by glowing red strips on the floor, pulsing faintly like a heartbeat. The faint hum of electronics filled the air, a subtle reminder that this place was as much about precision data as it was old-fashioned marksmanship. Targets hung at varying distances, from the casual ease of 1000 feet where hitting bullseyes was more about confidence than skill to the almost impossible challenge of 3000 feet away, where the targets flickered like shadows on the edge of a dream.

Langichatte LaBond stepped into the range, the odd man out in his own story. His gloves were the wrong kind entirely chunky, insulated, and designed more for keeping hands warm in a snowstorm than for trigger finesse.

"Precision, huh? They say it's about control. Me? I say precision is about intimacy. You and the bullet you talk. You vibe."

He swaggered toward his lane, the cold rubber mat beneath his feet contrasting with the warm confidence radiating from him. His footsteps echoed softly but steadily. Approaching the 1000-foot target, he took a slow, deep breath, inhaling the metallic scent of gun oil and polished brass.

Instructor (leaning back with boredom, voice low and flat):

"Standard M24 sniper weapon. No rapid fire. Focus on accuracy."

Langichatte smirked, barely suppressing a chuckle. He squared his shoulders, looking down the barrel as if he were greeting an old friend.

(mock serious):

"Do I look like I pray only on Sundays? Nah. I seduce the bullet. I romance the recoil."

He raised the weapon, finger resting lightly on the trigger, and squeezed.

BANG.

The shot rang out sharp and clean, the bullet punching a perfect hole right in the center of the bullseye.

BANG.

Again, a perfect strike.

BANG.

A third shot, no different. Three shots, three perfect bullseyes.

Langichatte (turning with a triumphant grin, addressing the other recruits):

"You, see? Me and the gun we're like lovers. We understand each other. This is what Haitians call 'Mwen pa nan jwet. I'm no joke."

The other trainees exchanged glances. A few nodded appreciatively. Some tried not to look impressed, but Langichatte caught the flicker of grudging respect in their eyes.

But the mood shifted quickly as the next challenge was announced: the 3000-feet shot. In Haiti LaBond never practice any shot pass 1000 foot. This experience was going to be new to him.

Langichatte narrowed his eyes, shifting his stance into something more serious. This wasn't the friendly kiss of mid-range fire. This was a test of nerves, skill, and luck. He controlled his breath, exhaling slowly, steadying the M24 in his hands.

BANG.

The bullet soared, but instead of hitting the target dead center, it veered sharply off course, ricocheting wildly. It slammed smack into one of the cadet's lunchboxes they place on the field to eat at lunch time.

Agent (shouting, panicked):

"Who fired at my lunch!?"

Cheeks flushed red, Langichatte look at the cadet and said "Don't shoot the messenger. God just used me to tell you to stop eating food with no seasoning. You need more Caribbean food in your life. Look at you… you pale." The cadet tried to reply but Langichatte shush and dismiss him while repositioning himself and took aim again.

BANG.

This time, the bullet etched a bizarre smiley face into the corner of the target board. It looked less like a mark of skill and more like a desperate plea a cry for help from the chaos of missed shots.

Instructor (deadpan, shaking his head):

"He's got the accuracy of a toddler with a crayon."

Langichatte sighed, lowering the M24.

Langichatte (half to himself, half sarcastic):

"Maybe I should've brought my slingshot. Or a rock."

Agent Carmichael, standing nearby with her digital tablet, made a few notes and added three glaring red flags to his file. One bluntly labeled: "Artistic but ineffective."

The Long Road to Precision

Langichatte's confidence from the mid-range shots quickly deflated under the weight of long-distance reality. It wasn't just about pulling the trigger anymore; it was about understanding wind speed, bullet drop, the subtle movements that could turn a clean shot into a disaster.

As the morning dragged on, the training became relentless. Langichatte ran through drills that required patience and near-perfect form, standing perfectly still as he took aim, feeling the cold metal of the M24 against his sweaty palms.

He tried focusing on the hum of the machines, the rhythm of his breathing, the flicker of the distant targets. But his mind kept wandering to the dusty streets of Port-au-Prince, to the smell of salt air by the coast, to the rhythm of Haitian drums in the night.

Each missed shot was a small stab in his pride, a reminder that talent wasn't enough. Skill was forged in repetition and discipline and sometimes, even that wasn't enough.

During a rare break, Langichatte retreated to the sidelines, nursing his bruised ego and his still-wobbly hands. He looked around and noticed Agent Carmichael watching him, her usual stoic expression softened just a fraction.

(approaching, voice low):

"Look, LaBond. Shooting isn't about flair or poetry. It's about control. Steady hands, clear mind. You have the instincts. You just need to learn how to channel them."

Langichatte (dry smile):

"And you think I'm channeling anything right now besides bad luck?"

She smiled a quick, almost imperceptible curve of her lips.

"You'll get there. But you need to stop trying to seduce the bullet and start listening to it."

Langichatte considered her words, folding his arms beneath his foil blanket as the cold settled back in.

"Listening, huh? Sounds easier than it is."

Return to the Line

When the session resumed, Langichatte took Carmichael's advice to heart. He slowed his breathing, steadied his grip, and focused on the faint hum in the air, the soft click of the weapon's mechanism.

He took aim again.

BANG.

Closer this time.

BANG.

Even closer.

BANG.

A shaky bullseye.

Langichatte felt a flicker of hope a quiet victory whispered in the language of marksmen.

Aftermath

When the session finally ended, the trainees gathered their gear and filed out of the range. Langichatte remained for a moment, staring down the rows of targets now peppered with his colorful failures and small successes.

Agent Carmichael approached once more.

"Not bad, LaBond. You might not be the sniper we hoped for, but you're not the 'Sniper of Sadness' either."

Langichatte (grinning tiredly):

"Guess, maybe, I'm the 'Sniper of… Rien de rien.'"

She laughed softly, LaBond's voice reminds her so much of her ex-boyfriend and it felt like a rare warmth was breaking through her morning chill.

Langichatte gathered his things. (quietly to himself):

"One day, me and that bullet we'll be speaking the same language."

Day 3: Defensive Driving – "The Mudslide Sonata"

The training track outside Echo-9 looked like the world's worst theme park ride designed by someone who hated fun. Tires, blackened and weather-beaten, were stacked haphazardly to create fake alleyways, tight corners, and dead ends. Rusted barrels leaked mysterious stains, some smoldering with small fires that curled wisps of smoke into the crisp morning air.

Mannequins dressed as civilians popped up without warning from behind corners or between obstacles, frozen mid-step with painted-on expressions ranging from casual curiosity to sheer panic. Above, drones buzzed relentlessly, circling like mechanical hawks capturing every angle, every mistake.

At the heart of this chaos stood a narrow bridge suspended precariously over a murky mud pit, the kind of pit that seemed ready to swallow cars whole. The bridge was no wider than a single car, its edges marked by faded yellow lines barely visible beneath a slick coating of grime. There was zero room for error one miscalculation, one slip, and the vehicle would plunge into the muck below. No safety nets, no second chances.

Langichatte LaBond approached the driver's door of the battered training car with the cautious optimism of a man who had just watched an action racing movie and believed, for one fleeting moment, that destiny was on his side.

He slid into the driver's seat like a man greeting an old, unreliable friend. He adjusted the seat, clicked the seatbelt with a satisfying snap, and tapped the dashboard affectionately.

(grinning, speaking softly to the car):

"You carry me, I carry you. You flip, I flip. We're in this together, mon ami."

The engine rumbled beneath him, a growl that promised speed and survival. Langichatte gripped the steering wheel, his knuckles whitening as he prepared to dance with danger.

He slammed his foot down on the gas.

SCREECH!

The tires screamed against the asphalt, the car launching forward like a bullet from a cannon.

The first half of the course was a blur. Langichatte weaved through the stacked tires with surprising finesse, drifting around corners like he'd been trained by a ghost from Tokyo Drift itself. His reflexes kicked in naturally, dodging the mannequin "civilians" with a grace that belied his earlier missteps in training. At one point, he executed a sharp handbrake turn that spun the car almost completely sideways. A cheer erupted from the watching recruits, some clapping, others whistling, surprised by his boldness.

Langichatte (pumped up, shouting over the roar):

"See? I got this! Caribbean style!"

But then... the bridge loomed ahead.

He slowed just a fraction, his eyes narrowing as he stared down the narrow strip like it had personally insulted his mother.

(whispering under his breath,):

"Y'all ever played Mario Kart without a reset button? Well, I'm so good in driving, no gas, I'll put mystery liquid boys on motorcycles give me, and still get where I need to get too. Watch me Nae Nae."

The car crept onto the bridge, each inch taken with the delicacy of a tightrope walker. The mud pit yawned beneath him, black and still, waiting.

Langichatte hit the gas, heart pounding, the car surging forward with a speed that blurred the edges of his vision.

WHAM.

CRUNCH.

SKID.

The rear wheel clipped the bridge's edge. The sound was a sickening scrape, metal grinding against concrete. The car tilted dangerously, the world seeming to slow in unbearable detail. Then, as if gravity itself was mocking him, the car slipped off the edge.

It tumbled and slid, a falling biscuit in slow motion, down into the waiting mud pit. The water erupted in a splash of brown and grime, soaking everything in a thick, clinging sludge.

Above, the drones buzzed closer, capturing the entire descent in cinematic slow motion the car's helpless plunge, the muffled sound of impact, the spray of mud.

Langichatte emerged from the wreckage like a defeated gladiator after a battle with gelatinous dessert. Mud coated his clothes, mud and grimed plastered on his forehead, and face.

He wiped the sludge from his eyes and took a deep breath.

(sputtering, voice dripping with bitter humor):

"Next time, I walk. Or Uber Black."

The recruits around the course laughed and clapped, some in disbelief, some in camaraderie. Even the instructors exchanged amused glances. The lesson was clear: even the best intentions could crash spectacularly.

Langichatte climbed out of the car, his legs shaking but his spirit strangely unbroken. He might not have conquered the Mudslide Sonata today, but he was learning sometimes the hard way how to survive it.

Day 4: The Swim Test – "Frozen Regret"

The Olympic-sized pool was a flawless rectangle of cold blue glass, nestled inside the Echo-9 facility like a jewel in a fortress. Its surface lay still and undisturbed, a mirror reflecting the harsh fluorescent lights above and the sterile white walls around. The edges were perfectly lined with white tiles, the faint scent of chlorine hanging in the air, a sharp contrast to the raw fear that gnawed at Langichatte's gut.

The pool looked beautiful. Clear. Still. Calm.

Also, demonic.

Langichatte stood at the edge, wrapped tightly in a towel that did little to shield him from the creeping chill that crawled beneath his skin. His muscles twitched involuntarily, and his jaw was clenched so hard it felt like his teeth might crack. He looked like a statue carved from frozen dread, his brown eyes fixed on the liquid abyss that awaited him below.

The water temperature read 65°F on a digital display nearby just shy of freezing in a way that felt like a personal betrayal. This wasn't the warm, soothing ocean that anyone could find and lap in the shores of Haiti's paradise. No, this was something else. Cold, unyielding, merciless.

The instructor, a tall woman with sharp eyes and a voice like steel, stood opposite him. She wore a tight wetsuit and held a stopwatch like a weapon.

Instructor (firm, no-nonsense):

"Twenty laps. No floating. No excuses. Go."

Langichatte blinked and swallowed hard, his throat dry.

He gingerly lifted one foot and dipped a single toe into the water.

The re-action was immediate.

SCREEEEEEAM.

Birds in the nearby trees scattered in startled flight. Somewhere behind him, a trainee dropped his protein shake with a loud clatter. A whisper floated through the air: "Is he being electrocuted?"

Langichatte's entire body seized as the cold water wrapped around his toe like icy fingers squeezing the life from him. He staggered back, shaking violently.

(voice trembling, almost pleading):

"This water is cursed. I swear to you, my grandmother warned me about this exact temperature. She said, 'Langichatte, if the water stings your soul it's not meant for you.'"

The instructor's brow furrowed, clearly unimpressed.

(fed up, tone clipped):

"It's water. Get into the pool."

Langichatte shook his head, retreating a few steps.

(almost desperate):

"This is not water. This is ocean trauma in a pool. I wouldn't even soak my socks in there. Not even the ones I hate."

He threw his towel around his shoulders like a shield and turned away from the pool, his posture crumpling with the weight of defeat. He walked with the dignity of a man who knew his limits and who had no intention of dying cold and soggy.

(shouting as he retreated):

"This is not swimming! This is marine punishment! I AM A TROPICAL BEING!"

Behind him, a smattering of laughter rose among the recruits half amused, half sympathetic. Agent Carmichael gave a knowing glance, as if he needs her in his life.

"LaBond, get into the pool right now cadet. That's an order."

He thought back to his childhood in Haiti, where swimming was a rite of passage warm seas under the sun, the taste of salt in the air, and the gentle embrace of the Caribbean waves. That water had been life itself, not this icy torment. He had loved the ocean like an old friend, and it had loved him back.

But this this sterile pool at Echo-9 felt like an adversary.

He glanced around the room and noticed the other recruits. Some were already in their lanes, diving smoothly and cutting through the water with practiced ease. Their faces were calm, focused, hardened by training Langichatte hadn't yet mastered.

One recruit, a lithe woman with determined eyes, swam past him, casting a glance of quiet encouragement. Langichatte nodded faintly, appreciating the gesture but feeling miles away from that confidence. Carmichael wasn't too please by her action.

"Look at this one. She's swimming in biofiltered pool, yet she's still thirsty."

Langichatte stopped pacing and looked back at the pool. The water seemed to mock him, serene and untouchable.

A cold breath escaped his lips.

Maybe I can do this.

He wiped his face with the towel and squared his shoulders.

(to himself, quietly):

"Okay, Langichatte. You're not just a tourist in this cold place. You're a fighter. You're a survivor. You've faced storms stronger than this."

He took a slow, deep breath, steadying his racing heart.

Without hesitation, he dropped the towel and approached the pool again.

The cold air bit at his skin as he lowered himself into the water, inch by inch. The chill hit him full force, a shock that took his breath away and left him gasping.

His skin prickled, and his teeth clenched.

(murmuring):

"Ammweyyyy, remember the sun... remember the warmth..."

The Struggle in the Water

The first lap was agony. Every stroke felt like dragging through ice. His limbs felt sluggish, his muscles reluctant to obey. His breath came fast and shallow, the cold seizing his lungs like a vise.

But he pushed on.

The second lap blurred into the third. His mind screamed to stop, to surrender, but his body moved on, driven by stubbornness and the faint memory of tropical tides.

Langichatte's vision narrowed, focusing on the black line at the pool's bottom guiding his path. Each pull of the arm, each kick of the leg, was a battle against the cold, against the numbness creeping up from his fingertips.

The instructor paced the poolside, stopwatch in hand, expression unreadable but unyielding.

Mental Warfare

Langichatte's mind wavered between despair and determination.

Why did I agree to this?

What was I thinking?

Carmichael to herself, "he needs me."

As he rounded the turn at the tenth lap, Langichatte heard a soft splash from the lane next to him. It was Carmichael, swimming effortlessly, her strokes precise and steady.

She slowed slightly, matching his pace.

Langichatte glanced sideways.

Agent Carmichael (quietly):

"Keep going. You're doing better than you think."

Her words were a lifeline, a small beacon of warmth in the cold water.

Langichatte nodded, fighting back a shiver.

Together, they swam two different worlds united in the same relentless pool.

The Final Push

With just a few laps left, Langichatte felt exhaustion clawing at him, but surrender was not an option.

He focused on the finish line, the imagined warmth waiting for him at the edge.

His strokes became more determined, more purposeful.

Finally, with the last powerful kick, he reached the pool's edge.

He hauled himself out, gasping and shivering but victorious.

Aftermath

Wrapped again in a towel, Langichatte's teeth still chattered, but his eyes held a spark of triumph.

Instructor (nodding approvingly):

"Not bad, LaBond. Not bad at all."

Langichatte (breathless, half-smiling):

"Next time... maybe the water will feel like home."

The recruits around him offered quiet applause, and Agent Carmichael... She, just smiled.

Langichatte looked at the pool one last time.

(softly):

"Frozen regret, maybe. But I survived."

FBI Operations Command, Washington, D.C

9:27 AM

The morning sun spilled cold light across the glass towers of downtown D.C., but inside the FBI Operations Command center, the atmosphere was thick with tension and stale coffee. On the forty-third floor, behind a soundproof wall of reinforced glass, sat Director Evelyn Sharpe.

Her office was a study in minimalism and quiet authority no nonsense, no decoration save for two American flags standing guard in opposite corners, and a jade bonsai tree that had somehow survived decades of federal bureaucracy, tended meticulously since the Bush administration.

The bonsai's miniature leaves shimmered under the harsh LED lights as Sharpe's eyes rested on the manila folder spread before her, labeled in bold black marker:

"LANGICHATTE LABOND – FIELD REVIEW"

She had reviewed that folder more times than she cared to admit. The contents were a perfect storm of comedy, catastrophe, and caffeine-fueled complaint memos.

It read like a black comedy script: a man who had failed every conceivable evaluation, who seemed more inclined to stumble into mishaps than avoid them, and yet somehow remained a fixture in the program.

Sharpe was a woman of few expressions, and fewer friends. Her jaw was permanently clenched as if she was holding back a storm inside. Her tailored blazer was so stiff and sharp-edged it could probably stop a bullet. It was her armor. She tapped the red rotary-style secure phone on her desk, took a slow, controlled breath, and dialed.

Ring.

Ring.

Ring.

Click.

A loud crunching noise, followed by clear chewing.

"Hello? Port-au-Prince Police, Captain Laurore speaking. If this is about the goat on Rue O, we already dealt with it," came the muffled voice.

Sharpe's eyes narrowed, but her tone remained clipped, professional.

"Captain Conrad Laurore. This is Director Sharpe, FBI Special Operations. I'm calling about your agent, Langichatte LaBond."

"Ahhh, Langichatte. Star of justice. My golden hurricane. My mango in a thunderstorm," Laurore replied cheerfully, still clearly chewing.

Sharpe blinked. Slowly. The absurdity hit her like a slap.

"He's failed every single qualifying evaluation," Sharpe said flatly. "He is unfit for the field. He poses a security liability. We are preparing to send him back."

There was a brief pause, then Captain Laurore's voice returned, bright as a tropical morning.

"Send him back? Oh no no no. You must not do that."

Sharpe raised an eyebrow but held steady.

"With all due respect, Captain, he couldn't swim, can't shoot past one thousand feet, and his hand-to-hand combat resulted in a dislocated ego and three viral YouTube compilations. All the other missions will fail, if we can't even get Father Zulu's baby brother."

Captain Laurore's voice turned conspiratorial.

"Yes, yes. But he has something you can't measure with tape or tests."

Sharpe's tone sharpened.

"Oh? And what's that? Delusion?"

There was a moment of static, then Conrad Laurore pretended to struggle with the line.

"Ahh! Hello? Hello? You said you love him? Yes, yes, I agree! He's very lovable."

Sharpe's teeth clenched.

"I said he is not qualified to continue the mission."

Captain Laurore's voice suddenly grew louder, filled with mock urgency.

"YOU SAID HE'S ESSENTIAL? OH YES, YES! ESSENTIAL! That's exactly the word I'd use. Essential like... seasoning! You can't make stew without spice, Director!"

Sharpe narrowed her eyes, recognizing the tactic immediately. She'd seen it before: weaponizing incompetence with charm. It was a rare and frustrating form of political manipulation.

"Captain Conrad Laurore. This is a federal task force. Not a food truck reality show."

"Signal is very bad here! You're breaking up! But I got your message loud and clear: Langichatte must finish his mission. Loud and clear! God bless America! Bye-bye!"

Click.

Dead silence.

Sharpe lowered the phone carefully, her fingers hovering over the disconnect button like she was considering calling back just to scream. Instead, she calmly shut the folder and stared out the window. The city stretched endlessly below her powerful, indifferent, relentless.

A gentle knock came at her door. A junior analyst poked his head in.

"Ma'am? Shall I keep Langichatte's status to 'Active Observer Special Circumstances'?"

Sharpe exhaled deeply, the sound long and weary, as if she were exorcising regret.

"He's going to survive for now on politics and pity. But this game is played with real bullets, that's going to get him killed."

The Folder: A Comedy of Errors

Sharpe's gaze drifted back to the folder now closed on her desk. Inside, the reports and evaluations painted a portrait of a man who was, at best, an enigma.

Sharpe rubbed her temples as she recalled the call with Captain Laurore. She had no patience for sentimental politics especially when national security was at stake. But Langichatte was a delicate diplomatic balancing act.

Port-au-Prince insisted on keeping their "golden hurricane" on this joint operation, and Washington was stuck in a quagmire of political correctness, local pride, and the occasional oddball agent who somehow grew on people.

Sharpe understood the stakes. Langichatte wasn't just a liability; he was a symbol. To the Haitian authorities, he represented hope, connection, and trust. To the FBI, he was a problem they had to manage delicately.

Her orders were clear: keep him out of the field and send him back to Haiti. But Captain Conrad Laurore's insistence had thrown a wrench into the plan.

A Quiet Moment

Sharpe's fingers traced the edge of the bonsai's tiny leaves.

Maybe she thought, there's something to this Langichatte after all. Something more than the mess in these reports.

But hope was not a luxury in her line of work.

She picked up her coffee cup, took a slow sip, and prepared to brief the higher-up's. The Langichatte dilemma was far from over.

"Looks like I have to call the Florida Director, Agent Gil and give him the bad news. Against our better judgment LaBond must go undercover without a real safety net in place. I, just hope he can prove all of us wrong."

Act 2
Infiltrating the Underworld

CHAPTER 4
UNDERCOVER IN FLORIDA

Private Marina, Miami Coastline
Golden Hour

The Miami skyline was melting in gold.

As the sun made its theatrical descent behind the chrome-glass towers, the city looked less like a place built by men and more like a golden hallucination. The marina, nestled in a secure inlet far from tourist noise, was unusually quiet the kind of quiet that costs money.

The yachts docked along the edges were imposing, but none dared match the audacity of the leviathan moored at the end of the most private pier. Her name was stenciled in gold script across her bow: The Narcotic Dream

She didn't just float. She reigned.

The entire upper deck was alive with elegance soft jazz music floated through hidden speakers, mingling with the lazy laughter of the already inebriated and the calculating silence of the soberly dangerous.

String lights crisscrossed overhead in golden arcs, blinking like fireflies on cue. Exotic plants in ceramic pots whispered in the ocean breeze. And guards with the muscles of rugby teams stood near entrances, pretending to look bored.

Every guest seemed to have stepped out of an unspoken fashion agreement: tailored tuxedos, sapphire cufflinks, gowns that clung like secrets, and enough glittering jewelry to blind passing seagulls.

The air itself was thicker than the humidity it was curated. A rich bouquet of $500 cigars, hand-rolled in countries not found on maps, mingled with amber perfumes, oud colognes, and the exotic, sweet punch of pomegranate-mint hookah smoke. Beneath it all was a metallic undercurrent: the cold scent of gun oil and risk.

Then came a small disturbance in this scented sea of wealth a flash of floral panic and charm.

Langichatte LaBond had arrived.

Langichatte stood at the edge of the pier, eyeing The Narcotic Dream like she was a too-fancy date he couldn't afford but was going to impress anyway.

His red tuxedo, freshly pressed and straight from tailor Rony Pierre Desnisca from Port-au-Prince, was a thing of local beauty crafted with care, love, and his signature three-quarter length pants.

Beads of sweat formed on his brow with the urgency of a military operation. His armpits were locked in combat. Still, he stood tall chin up, shoulders back, adjusting his tie with a perfect Windsor knotted backward like he was Mac Daddy himself from Kris Kross.

(to himself, whispering):

"Alright, Langichatte. Walk cool. Don't slip. Don't sweat like a boiled yam."

Still, he pressed forward, marching toward the boarding ramp with the confident gait of a man who knew exactly how out of place he was but refused to show it.

The Boarding Ramp

At the base of the ramp stood a woman who looked like she had been grown in a lab to sell perfume. She wore a form-fitting black dress with a slit so high it almost counted as a biography. Her earpiece blinked once every few seconds. She was tall. Symmetrical. The kind of symmetrical that came with invoices.

Hostess (with zero facial emotion):

"Welcome aboard, Mr…?"

shaking her head slightly, as she waits for LaBond to tell her his name.

Langichatte paused dramatically, and flashed a grin that could melt sunscreen.

"LaBond. Langichatte LaBond."

He took her hand, kissed the air above it, and let a faint cloud of mango body oil trail in his wake like a signature fragrance only found in one part of the Caribbean.

She typed his name into a sleek, futuristic tablet. Her smile remained professional, just a millimeter too practiced to be real.

Hostess:

"Right this way, Mr. LaBond. The tournament is about to begin. I will let the organizers know our final contestant has just arrive."

As he stepped up the ramp, Langichatte let himself soak it in. All of it.

The sounds, the scents, the feeling of luxury that wasn't quite welcoming it was judging. Judging your posture. Judging your drink. Judging your bloodline.

On Deck: A Parade of Power

The moment his feet touched the teak deck, Langichatte paused.

The floor itself seemed to hum under his soles. Polished teak inlaid with swirling ivory designs, each plank lacquered to a mirror shine. Every detail from the golden railings to the potted bonsai trees trimmed to perfection whispered: this is not for you.

(to himself):

"If Haiti had a yacht like this, we'd sail it straight to France and ask for back pay. At the very least 300 billion dollars' worth."

Waiters in crisp, white jackets moved with graceful precision, carrying silver trays of crystal flutes, gold-leaf canapés, and things that looked expensive but smelled like refrigerated sea creatures.

A particularly confident waiter approached with a tray of bubblies balanced in one hand like he was a performer from cirque du soleil.

Waiter:

"Champagne, sir?"

Langichatte (shaking his head politely):

"No no no. I prefer my drinks without bubbles and my decisions with clarity."

He made a discreet beeline to the bar, ignoring the cluster of guests who gave him a once-over and whispered behind designer sunglasses. He could feel their eyes, not in anger, but curiosity.

He didn't look like old money. He didn't smell like foreign oil. He wasn't oozing with cocaine wealth or bling out like an Eastern European warlord.

He looked like someone who was either very dangerous... or very lost.

From this vantage point, he scanned the crowd again memorizing faces, noting exits, and reminding himself that everyone here, no matter how elegant, had blood on their money.

And at the far end of the deck, beneath the soft spotlight and beside a velvet rope, a new chapter awaited.

Behind the glowing onyx counter stood a bartender who looked like a young Isaac from The Love Boat. Just by looking at him, you can tell his mixed drinks are made by natural instinct and each one are work of arts.

Bartender:

"What'll it be, sir?"

Langichatte leaned against the bar with practiced swagger.

"I'll have a virgin mango smoothie. Shaken. No ice."

The bartender blinked.

"Did I hear you right, a virgin mango smoothie"

Langichatte:

"Yes, absolutely. I prefer my courage sober and my taste tropical."

The bartender looked momentarily offended, then intrigued.

Now excited to take on the task:

"Alright then. One virgin mango smoothie, shaken. No ice."

Langichatte took his drink and sipped with pleasure. The sweetness cut through the thick atmosphere like a machete through sugarcane. He turned to watch the crowd. Every guest was a story wrapped in silk and diamonds, and every smile hid a secret. These weren't just gamblers they were traffickers, arms dealers, crypto laundering tycoons. All here for one thing: a chance at a $25 million payday and under-the-table favors from ZoGod himself.

Aboard The Narcotic Dream– Middle Deck Entrance to Casino Hall

The velvet rope separating the upper deck from the inner sanctum of the casino wasn't just there for security it was a symbolic barrier. A shimmering red thread that divided the rich from the ruthlessly rich, the players from the power brokers.

At its center stood Rose, a statuesque Haitian Supermodel with piercing hazel eyes, dressed in a silver gown that shimmered like mercury. The gown hugged her like a contract with consequences. Her high cheekbones, sharp enough to violate international airspace, reflected the soft lighting as if daring it to catch up. She closely resembles a young Angela Bassett

Behind her sat a black lacquered table so minimalist it looked sculpted from obsidian. A small biometric scanner pulsed gently with blue light. The buy-in terminal displayed the current pot:

"$49,000,000 49 out of 50 check-in."

Rose glanced up from her tablet as Langichatte LaBond strolled toward her, tropical smoothie in hand, strutting like the red carpet had just appeared under his feet by divine decree.

His tuxedo, slightly damp from sweat, still managed to catch the light like it was made of moonlight and stolen casino chips. He took a final sip from the straw and smiled like he had just remembered a joke only rich people could afford to laugh at.

Rose (without warmth):

"We been expecting you. The buy-in is one million."

Langichatte stopped short. His brows raised, and he drew back slightly, eyes wide in mock offense.

(with an incredulous chuckle and his FBI credit card in his wallet):

"Really? That's all?"

He reached into his jacket pocket with a flourish as if about to produce a rabbit or a diplomatic immunity document. Instead, he revealed a matte black credit card, its surface unbranded, its chip gold. It gave off the kind of soft gleam that said: This card doesn't just buy luxury it funds governments.

Langichatte (smiling, extending the card):

"Here you go, sweetheart. And take ten percent as your tip. For the ambiance."

Rose looked at the card but didn't take it right away. Her eyes scanned his face first, as if searching for signs of delusion or bravado. Then she took the card and slid it through the scanner with the same expression one might use while checking for counterfeit bills.

DING.

The terminal chirped pleasantly. A green glow confirmed the transaction.

(handing back the card, flatly):

"Thank you. But unnecessary."

Her tone was polite but frosty. Langichatte's smile widened, undeterred.

Rose (eyes flicking to her tablet):

"Is there a preferred name or nickname you would like to be identified by?"

(with practiced flair)

"No. just my actual name. LaBond. Langichatte LaBond."

There was a pause. Her expression didn't change, but the silence around her seemed to grow a little thicker. Like the air knew, he wasn't supposed to be here.

Rose (with the faintest tilt of her head):

"Nice meeting you, Langichatte LaBond."

She slid her finger across her tablet, completing the entry. The velvet rope unclipped with a mechanical click, slowly retracting like the drawbridge of a digital castle.

Rose (neutral, but with a glint of challenge):

"I'd wish you good luck in this tournament... but ZoGod has won seven years in a row."

Langichatte's smile cooled slightly, but only slightly. He lifted his smoothie in a toast.

Rose (faint smile):

"So… you'll need more than luck."

Langichatte took a casual sip, letting the silence between them simmer.

 (lowering his glass):

"I'm Haitian. Luck is for people with no faith"

(Another pause. eyes twinkling):

"When you know you been chosen by a higher power since you been six years old. And he will use you as one of his servants to feed the hungry all over the world. You'll walk in every room already claiming victory."

Rose allowed herself the faintest curve of her lips. Not a smile, exactly more like acknowledgment. Like watching someone confidently walk into a lion's den wearing cologne made of steak juice.

She turned back to her terminal.

Langichatte adjusted his jacket, patted his chest twice, and strode past the rope with the stride of a man who didn't know the rules but planned to charm them into submission.

The entrance to the casino room whispered open with a hydraulic sigh, revealing a vision of engineered seduction and strategy.

The room was located on the lower deck, design language cathedral-like, with curved mahogany walls that seemed to trap sound in velvet. The air conditioning was cooler here deliberately, so the players stayed alert and the tension never broke a sweat. Overhead, a fiber-optic sky ceiling glimmered with simulated constellations that slowly shifted positions, creating the illusion of passing time without ever showing a clock.

In the center of it all sat five round poker tables, arranged like petals around a central hub. Spotlighting from the ceiling lit each table like a theatrical set. The carpet beneath was deep red and impossibly plush so soft it muffled footsteps like a spy film.

At the center table, exactly where one would expect the sun god to lounge in the middle of his universe, sat ZoGod.

He didn't look up as Langichatte entered. He didn't have to.

ZoGod was the kind of man who could command silence with his lounging posture. His silk shirt shimmered under the lights with shifting hues of sea green and blood red, like a reptile at peace after a meal. His fingers danced over a stack of engraved chips platinum and obsidian. His sunglasses were still on, even though there was no sunlight. He chewed something slowly maybe gum, maybe your future.

Langichatte was shown to Table Four not the center of the room, but close enough to feel the gravity of ZoGod's presence. He adjusted his cuffs, sat down, and took in the layout.

The cards were thick, weighted with gold foil edges. The chips bore the yacht's crest, and the dealers dressed in custom black suits might as well have been statues. Silent, efficient, soulless.

Langichatte casually slipped in his earpiece, the kind you wouldn't see unless you were actively looking inside someone's skull.

Agent Carmichael's voice came through like thunder wrapped in silk.

(through earpiece):

"Alright, sunshine. This is a 50-players battle rumble tournament. Winner takes half the pot. And get notice by ZoGod himself. You're in table 4, seat six. Seat three is a known bluffer. Seat seven had been kicked out of a few casinos for counting cards. And our trophy target ZoGod, prefers hyper-aggressive plays, so, let's make your present be known, so we can get invited to his table. But for now, let's focus on being the top 5 players on our table. Follow my lead. Your quirkiness is adorable if a strong woman likes those types of things but this is not the place for it, so please, don't embarrass us."

Langichatte muttered back softly, hiding his lips with a napkin.

(whispering):

"Oui, madam. I'll do my best not to embarrass you. My charm is my shield."

He leaned back and nodded, donning his most smug expression one part James Bond, two parts Haitian comedian SEJOE.

First Hands – Baptism by Bluff

The first hand dealt was clean. Langichatte peeked King and Queen of diamonds. Not bad.

He sipped his smoothie. Cool, unbothered.

Then he saw the flop: Ace, Jack, Ten all hearts.

He folded.

Carmichael (snapping):

"You had a straight, Langichatte! Why did you fold?"

Langichatte (shrugging):

"I had a bad feeling. And the smoothie was distracting. Tastes like pure addiction."

The very next hand, he was dealt a pair of twos. He smiled confidently. Raised the bet by $50,000. Several players folded. One tried to re-raise. Langichatte stared him down dramatically, then pushed all his chips forward.

Carmichael:

"What are you doing?! We're going to lose."

The player looks at LaBond for a while, thinking to himself- the game just started, and he wasn't prepared to go home as yet. So, he folded.

Langichatte won the hand.

(whispering):

"You, see? That's not poker. That's performance art.

Disaster and Recovery – My Haitian Ritual in Action"

On the other hand, Langichatte reached for his smoothie and managed to knock it directly into the lap of the Colombian enforcer Alberto with a scar down his cheek seated beside him a mountain of a man with tattoos that looked like confessionals.

The entire table froze.

Langichatte stood immediately, gasped like he had seen a ghost, as the Columbian enforcer gets up, furiously wanted to punch the living daylights out of him.

"OH! Forgive me, my brother! The spirit of my best friend Conrad Laurore wanted me to warn you; you have some evil spirit that's trying to kill you."

The man blinked. Langichatte took the cloth napkin and gave it to him, as Alberto exasperated, begin to carefully removing the stain off his pants, while still debating whether or not he should punch him. "Why would evil spirits want to kill me?".

"Why do evil wants to do evil? Those types of questions are impossible to answer." As LaBond is sizing up the Columbian enforcer by feeling on his biceps. They felt like rocks. LaBond wanted no part of this man. "I'm sensing you want to punch me right now." The Columbian replied "Yes, I do sense that desire is very strong in me." "See, you're worrying about the wrong thing. For your protection, I need you to repeat after me. Bondié sé papa mwen, soti sou mwen satan." The Columbian repeat it those words as instructed three times. "You just said in Creole that God is your father and so, Satan has no authority to even try to attempt to kill you. You must stop having anger in your heart. Evil will feed on that. Congratulations, you're saved."

The audience claps. ZoGod gets up and said "Enough, can we please go back to playing poker?" LaBond said "Of course" than he reach-out and took $100,000 worth of chips from the Enforcers pot. The Columbian grab LaBond's wrist "What gives?"

"I'm sorry, did I just save your life? Do you know how much of my energy was taken from me just now? Do you believe you can go and spend your wealth in the afterlife. Do you care to try?"

With undeniable logic, the Columbian sat back down to continue the game.

"You Haitians are crazy."

Langichatte (smiling):

"Yes, we are. But my friend, there's no stronger prayer than a Haitian mother praying for you."

The table roared with approve laughter. Even ZoGod, from his seat across the room, cracked a smile beneath his glasses. Cause even he knows, with all the things he's into. He's still alive because of his mother's prayers.

Langichatte sat down, made a hand signal to the bartender for a refill. Agent Carmichael muted the intercom as her eyes are lock on the camera feed. "Big head, you really like the taste of mangoes in your sweet palate. Don't you?". Agent Ben and Rogers just stayed quiet.

Hand after hand, players were eliminated. Some cursed in five languages. Others smiled grimly, tipped their dealers, and left the room as if someone had just informed them their yachts had exploded.

Langichatte played like a man in a fever dream. He bluffed high with garbage cards. He folded decent hands and dodged traps. Carmichael shouted in his ear; Langichatte ignored half of it and yet, he survived. Carmichael's emotions went on a roller-coaster that evening.

(grumbling through the static):

"You're either the luckiest moron I've ever seen or some kind of Haitian warlock. If you were next to me right now, I wouldn't know whether to kiss you or to choke you."

Langichatte:

"If it was up to me, I'll pick the kiss over the choke every time."

Agent Ben and Agent Rogers also assigned as shadow agents on the surveillance boat listening to everything on their headphones, gave each other a look. By the end of the first phase, the tension in the room had shifted. What started as snickers and sideways glances had morphed into wariness. Langichatte wasn't just surviving. He was climbing the ranks. By now all the strong players seems to notice each other. Even ZoGod gave LaBond a second look.

The drug lord had yet to speak a word, but his dealer Ti-Ruby has been working for him as a servant for close to ten years. With trembling hands kept dealing him suspiciously perfect hands. Langichatte noticed it. So did Carmichael.

"ZoGod just eliminated another player at his table. Dealer's feeding ZoGod. This is going to be a big problem for us to overcome when we get to the final table. But for now, just keep playing your game."

Langichatte adjusted his backward tie and smirked.

"Oh, I plan to. Let's see how long his luck holds."

The tournament room had quieted into a tense hum. The scent of adrenaline now mingled with the fading sharpness of victory and the quiet mourning of bankrolls vaporized.

LaBond just eliminated the 24th player of the evening. And not to be outdone Twitchy Man Forkan disposed of the 25th. The way Twitchy Man Forkan won that last hand felt questionable with ZoGod, so he called Rose over

Two and a half dozen had been whittled down in a gauntlet of high-stakes mind games and silent warfare across all five tables. And yet, Langichatte LaBond, babysitting his new glass of mango smoothie, poker face somewhere between smug and "I forgot the rules," was still very much in the game.

A soft chime echoed across the room. The lights subtly shifted from surgical white to a warmer amber.

Intercom (smooth, male, slightly eerie):

"Ladies and gentlemen, we will now break for the day. Twenty-five players remain. Please enjoy our hospitality. Round two will commence tomorrow. At an undisclosed time and location."

The message ended with a soft ding the kind that usually accompanied boarding instructions or doomsday announcements.

Players began to stand, stretch, and wander toward the bar or the outer deck. But the top 10 most dangerous players who possibly could end ZoGod's winning streak where conveniently "randomly" selected to be search.

Langichatte exhaled, leaned back, and began stretching like a man who had just escaped a shark tank with his limbs intact. His fingers cracked one by one.

(murmuring):

"Still alive. Still charming. Still feel so good in this 100% wool suit, it's so warm."

And then she appeared Rose, moving through the crowd with the grace of a panther in silk. Her dress had somehow become more shimmering since he'd last seen her. She walked like she owned the ocean. She stopped directly in front of Langichatte's table and gave him the kind of smile that could either melt your heart or signal a coming autopsy.

(smiling tightly):

"It seems like your faith and your mother's prayers has been working for you thus far, Mr. LaBond."

Langichatte (rising, stretching with a yawn):

"Your voice carries concerns. Is it presumptuous of me to notice?"

Rose (gesturing):

"I really wish I didn't have to do this. But I must do my job. Please. You need to come with me."

Langichatte froze for a split second. Just long enough to register the danger behind the hospitality.

Then his earpiece crackled.

Agent Carmichael (in his ear, voice tight):

"They're searching to see if anybody was cheating. Get rid of your earpiece right now. Be smart, do it fast."

Langichatte's eyes darted across the room. He spotted them instantly security men in tailored suits, splitting up, preparing to scan faces, moving with the slow inevitability of a storm front. Two people already blocked the main hallway. One was speaking into his wrist.

Then his eyes landed on a man at the next table. He was twitchy, mid-30s, dressed in a blue silk suit that screamed insecurity disguised as confidence. His eyes never stayed still. He scratched his arm too often. And most importantly, he hadn't lost a single hand all night.

Langichatte's brain clicked.

(to himself):

"Nervous hands. Perfect cards. That's not luck. That's cheating."

He stood casually and walked beside the man, brushing his shoulder.

Langichatte (grinning, patting him like an old friend):

"Hey! Long night, huh? You closed round 1 by sending the 25th player packing. It's a beautiful game played by beautiful people. Congratulations."

Twitchy Man Forkan blinked at LaBond, as he's showing off his sinister smile. He saw LaBond as a mark. He took the glasses he was using to count cards and slip it in Langichatte's suit pocket. Just as Langichatte was slipping his earpiece into the breast pocket of the man's coat.

Twitchy Man Forkan begin to sing for joy. "First, I was afraid. I was petrified. (He then sings the next line in a low tone holding his right hand next to his mouth close to LaBond's ear.) I did a little booboo at thought I would die. Because of you dear friend, I will survive, (regular tone) I will survive. (higher tone) I will Survive I WILL SURvivvvvveeee. HaHahahhahahaHA! Thank you. Let's just say, I kept my eyes on the prize."

Confused, LaBond clap anyway to blue slick suit man's performance. "As my favorite character Blaine Edwards would say, you got talent you go boy. You sexy and delicious Gazak you. Here's your like, act like I'm TravQue and walk away from me." And just like that, he walks away from him.

Rose, who had been watching, ask LaBond.

"Friend of yours?"

Langichatte (smiling easily):

"Briefly. Like most of my relationships."

Rose didn't laugh. She gestured again, and he followed, heart pounding beneath his fashion forward tie wearing style.

The lounge, once humming with whispers and quiet conversation, now felt like a courtroom seconds before the verdict.

The waitstaff had vanished, their silver trays and flutes of champagne replaced by the subtle click of boot heels on polished teak. Every exit is now guarded. The overhead lights dimmed just slightly, but it was enough to make the gold in the room look like it had lost confidence in itself.

Gone was the music that had gently laced the air with smooth jazz and tropical indulgence. It had been replaced by something ambient low, atonal, a heartbeat's echo slowed and stretched like rubber. The kind of background noise that made people forget how to breathe normally.

At the center of the room, in front of the floor-to-ceiling windows that framed the moonlit sea, the top 10 players were arranged in a line. While the other 15 stood and watch.

Their expressions ranged from indifference to icy calm to rising dread. A few looked insulted by the procedure. Others looked like they were doing math in their heads calculating the risk of concealment, the odds of survival.

Langichatte stood among them, third in line.

His arms were relaxed at his sides. His breathing is shallow. His smile was nowhere to be found. But inside, his thoughts were sprinting like rats in a sinking ship.

(internal):

"Okay. Easy now. They don't know. They didn't see you. No sweat well, okay, a little sweat. But not suspicious sweat. Natural sweat. Good sweat. Island sweat."

He adjusted his cuff slightly, resisting the urge to glance at the blue-suited man two spaces behind him.

A squad of four guards silent, in black tactical suits trimmed with gray moved with synced precision. Each held a sleek scanning device, shaped like a wand but moving with the deliberate authority of a scalpel.

The first player stepped forward a sharp-jawed Brit with mirrored sunglasses still on. The scanner swept his body from head to heel. No sound.

Beep. Green light.

He gave a sarcastic bow and stepped aside.

The second player, a statuesque woman in a red dress with a scar that peeked from behind her ear, followed. She showed her hands. Removed her earrings. Didn't blink once.

Beep. Green light.

She returned to her cocktail like nothing had happened.

Then it was LaBond's turn. Langichatte (smiling at the guard):

"First time anyone's touched me tonight. Try not to fall in love."

The guard didn't react. Just began the scan, moving from his head to his toes. A brief pat down followed behind the ears, under the arms, around the ankles.

Beep. Green light. Twitchy Man Forkan look confused. He knew he place his illegal glasses in LaBond's suit. How could he receive a green light? He thought to himself, as he quickly started to search his own pockets for any illegal items.

By the time he realized the illegal glasses was back in his pockets. It was his turned to be search. He quickly acted like he was sneezing and place the glasses in one of the securities guard's pockets with a $50,000 chip. The guard check his pockets and saw both items. He thought to himself for a few seconds. Twitchy Man Forkan in panic mode, folded his hands, as if to say please don't rat me out.

Langichatte barely turned his head, but his peripheral vision sharpened like a hawk's. The man's movements were fidgety. He wiped his palms on his jacket. The security guard place his hand on Twitchy Man Forkan's shoulder as if to say I accept your offer, but you need to relax or you're going to get both of us in trouble. "Please raise your hands, so I can search you.".

Grateful, he confidently raises his hands. The scanner passed once over his chest.

BEEP.

The sound wasn't loud. But in that silence, it might as well have been a gunshot.

Everyone stiffened.

The guard narrowed his eyes. Ran the wand back over the same spot.

BEEP.

Twitchy Man Forkan's voice cracked like old floorboards.

(nervous laugh):

"I have a pacemaker. Yeah. That's what it is. Medical. Yes, it's a medical device for my poor heart."

The guard tilted his head, as if to say how silly are you? Why you didn't warn me you had another device in your possession. Now, I can't help you, everybody's watching. Slowly, he reached toward the man's coat pocket and pulled out the tiny matte-black

earpiece the one Langichatte had slipped in minutes earlier. Now his somewhat feeling bad, knowing this man's life is going to be unalive for cheating by ZoGod.

The room froze.

Breathing stopped. Blinks were missed. Even the ambient hum from the speakers seemed to pause in anticipation.

Langichatte felt a shiver crawl down his spine not from guilt, but from sheer awareness if he didn't think fast on his feet, this could've been his moment.

Security Lead (calm, deliberate):

"What is this?"

Twitchy Man Forkan started having anxiety attack. (panic blooming):

"That's not mine! I I don't know how that got there! I swear! I swear on my kids, my mom, my dog ZoGod knows me. I'm a very good friend of his."

He was babbling now. Too fast. Too loud. The kind of panic that people only exhibit when they know their fate is sealed and no one's going to stop it.

Two new figures entered from the shadowed alcove near the stairwell. Both wore navy suits, gold lightning bolt pins, and expressions so neutral they bordered on robotic. Their steps were too quiet. Their gazes too flat.

They didn't speak.

They didn't need to.

Each grabbed one of Twitchy Man Forkan's arms, gently but firmly, and turned him toward a side door no one had noticed before. Twitchy Man Forkan tried to protest, twisting as he walked. While begging for mercy.

"Wait! Wait! I swear! I was framed! Someone planted that on me! This is a mistake! ZoGod knows me. We party every weekend."

No one moved. No one looked at Langichatte.

The guards opened the door as the security guard who initially check Twitchy Man Forkan quietly follow them, two steps behind. A soft light spilled out for a second, framing the man's panicked silhouette.

Then Click.

The door closed. The lock turned.

Three beats of silence.

Then A distant splash.

Not a scream. Just a splash in the middle of international waters. As the two enforcers walk away, the security guard look for a lifeline flotation vest and threw it at the sea, hoping Twitchy Man Forkan finds it.

Final. Cold, that's all the security guard could have done. Anything more than that, and he would place himself in harm's way. Let's just hope the sea, don't do its ancient work in modern times.

Langichatte's hand tightened briefly around the edge of the nearby table.

(internally):

"You made it out. You made it through. But don't think for one second that you're safe."

He forced his shoulders to relax. Straightened his spine. Returned his expression to its default setting: nonchalant confidence with a hint of mango mystery.

A few of the players exchanged glances. Others turned away, uninterested. But the message had been received by everyone in the room.

No cheating. No exceptions. No second chances.

The silence lingered like smoke. Even after the splash had faded into memory, its ghost remained, haunting the room in the tremble of breath and the cautious shuffle of a shoe. Conversations didn't resume. Nobody laughed. Nobody reached for their drinks.

The rest of the players were search, but nothing eventful happened.

Then, cutting through the stillness like a silver blade, came Rose's voice.

Rose (cool and deliberate):

"We apologize for the disruption. You are free to move about the yacht. However,"

She paused, letting the weight settle before delivering the final strike.

"Tampering with the game will not be tolerated."

There was no drama. No threats. Just a simple truth, spoken like the rules of physics. Tamper, and you vanish. Everyone understood now.

Langichatte stood still, exhaling with a slow, deliberate rhythm the kind of exhale that only comes after not breathing for two full minutes. His knees still buzzed with the memory of proximity to death, but his face? Calm. Tranquil. Maybe even slightly amused.

He turned slowly toward the window, letting the soft, dappled light from the chandelier fall across his features as if he were in a commercial for the world's most stylish near-death experience.

(to self):

"Never trust a man with a twitch and perfect cards. And thank God I wore this wool suit, cause some nights really do get chilly."

As the players began to disperse some heading for the bar, others to quiet corners, Rose's heels clicked softly against the floor as she approached Langichatte. There was no urgency to her walk, but there was purpose.

She stopped two steps from him, her gaze as unreadable as ever. But something had shifted.

A new wariness. Maybe respect. Maybe suspicion.

(softly):

"Why do you move as if the world is yours."

Langichatte turned to face her, a faint smile playing at the edge of his lips. He lifted his glass, the condensation from his mango smoothie sliding down his fingers.

(quiet, sincere):

"I do believe you should blame Nas for that. Cause, he came out with a song of the same title in May 1994. And seeing him ether a takeover, I knew, if I work hard at it with belief in my heart, I could rule the world too."

She studied him for a moment longer. No smile. "Well, let's see if tomorrow can bring you the same type of faith you carry. Cause, you're going to need it."

Then, with a curt nod, she turned to speak with the Columbian enforcer Alberto and Swet Holedeuvi. "Mr. Holedeuvi, Alberto tells me, he's a big philanthropist. I think you two should get to know each other."

"That's very admirable, we need more people like you in this world." Swet replied.

Langichatte let out a breath he hadn't realized he was still holding and made his way to the bar.

The bar was quieter now. No more showy laughter or clinking champagne. Just low murmurs, cautious glances, and the bartender silently polishing a glass that had already been cleaned.

Langichatte slid onto a stool with the air of a man returning to his natural habitat. He tapped the counter twice.

"One more smoothie, please. Same thing. Virgin mango. Shaken. No ice. And… a small umbrella if you've got it."

The bartender didn't blink. He just nodded with two finger snap and a gun salute with each hand, and got to work.

Langichatte leaned forward, resting his elbows on the counter, the events of the last ten minutes replaying like a jazz riff with too much percussion. Every word. Every twitch. Every angle of every eye in the room.

The smoothie was placed in front of him. He lifted it in a small toast to himself, to the sea, to whichever angel from heaven that been protecting him so far.

(softly, with a smirk):

"One down. Twenty-four to go."

He sipped.

Focusing on the task at hand.

"Let's just hope their open bar, never runs out of mango."

He stared into the mirrored shelves behind the bar, where rows of glittering bottles sparkled like trophies. And in that reflection, he could see the players behind him moving, thinking, plotting. Some stared at him. Others are pretending not to.

He smiled at his reflection. Gave himself a wink.

And then, casually, he turned back to face the room.

CHAPTER 5
THE FINAL BLUFF

Undisclosed Beneath the sub-basement of a hotel and casino in Miami or Somewhere Far Worse

The last glimpse of moonlight disappeared behind velvet as black satin blindfolds were pulled snugly over every player's eyes.

No questions were asked. No instructions were offered. Only the soft-spoken usher, dressed in matte black, face expressionless, gave a single command:

"Remain still. Do not speak."

Langichatte, sandwiched between two players who smelled like cologne and betrayal, shifted slightly in his seat. He could feel the floor beneath him vibrating some kind of engine rumbling softly, as if the whole room were riding inside the belly of a mechanical beast.

It wasn't a car. It wasn't another boat. It was something else.

The journey was silent. Not even hushed whispers. Just the constant mechanical hum, the occasional metallic groan of reinforced steel adjusting under stress, and the steady clack-clack-clack of wheels or gears turning underneath them.

Langichatte tilted his head, trying to guess where he was being taken.

(thinking):

"I've been blindfolded before. That time with the Dominican twins and the broken elevator... but this feels less flirty and more... funeral."

Twenty-four players. Twenty-four hearts beating like buried clocks.

Then a sudden stop.

A door opened somewhere ahead. A rush of air, colder than expected, slipped into the space, smelling faintly of stone, cigar smoke, and a hint of lavender.

"Remove your blindfolds," came a voice over a hidden speaker. Polite. Crisp. British. And vaguely threatening, like a headmaster who owned a private army.

Langichatte pulled his blindfold down. And gasped.

Waiters in tuxedos drifted through the room carrying trays of aged whiskey, gold-leaf desserts, cigars stored in glass humidors, and champagne bottles that probably cost more than houses in Haiti.

Langichatte slowly turned in place, taking everything in, while adjusting his backward tie.

(murmuring)

"ZoGod doesn't host tournaments."

He glanced upward at the chandelier.

"He hosts The Wolf of Wall Street type parties. I'm not going nowhere."

Each player was handed a gold room key engraved with a gold tiger insignia.

A servant bowed politely.

"Please enjoy your quarters. The final round begins tomorrow evening."

Langichatte immediately turned toward Rose.

She stood beside ZoGod's security detail wearing shimmering silver, elegant enough to distract a priest during prayer.

Langichatte smiled.

"So… should I leave my room key with the front desk and be with you tonight. We can be roomies."

Rose stared at him for two full seconds.

Then smirked.

"Win the tournament first, Mr. LaBond."

She leaned closer.

"Then maybe I'll reward your confidence."

Langichatte pressed a hand dramatically to his chest.

"Woman, don't threaten me with happiness."

Rose rolled her eyes.

"Goodnight, Mr. LaBond."

Agent Carmichael now back at headquarters, writing out her report. Touch her computer screen where she wrote LaBond's name. "You're on your own now big head. Try not to die."

Next Day

The room was colossal longer than an Olympic stadium and sunken beneath what could only be described as a fortress. The walls were ancient limestone, weathered but polished, lined with ornate columns and torch-like sconces flickering with real flame.

And yet, everything gleamed with technology motion-triggered LED runners, magnetic sliding panels, and a central ceiling entirely made of crystal glass, above which an artificial sky projected stars, nebulas, and swirling galaxies.

It was like someone had fused a cathedral, a luxury bunker, and a Bond villain's wine cellar.

In the center of it all sat the poker floor five velvet-draped tables arranged beneath a chandelier made of crushed diamonds suspended in glass orbs, glowing with a golden pulse.

Red velvet curtains hung from the ceiling, rippling with unseen drafts. Waitstaff in tuxedos carried trays of rare liquors, gilded desserts, and cigars stored in humidified lockboxes.

Langichatte turned slowly in place, letting the scene soak in. Now wearing a blue suit from the same Haitian tailor Rony Pierre

(murmuring):

"All you have to do is win this tournament and she will be all yours. Sounds easy enough." Each table holding some of the most dangerous gamblers, criminals, financiers, assassins, and sociopaths on Earth.

And ZoGod's table?

It held the five lowest-ranked players by chip count.

The weak. The desperate. The disposable.

Everyone understood what that meant.

ZoGod didn't just want to win.

He wanted entertainment before execution.

The other four tables held the elite survivors: Colombian enforcer Alberto, The Killer Nun, Niko, the Japanese mob boss, A South African banker worth more than small countries. Scorpion, the silent assassin from Macau and somehow, Langichatte LaBond.

The dealers moved with robotic precision as cards slid across velvet like sharpened blades.

Then the overhead voice returned.

"Round One begins now."

The room fell silent.

Five Tables

Langichatte sat relaxed at Table One, sipping his mango smoothie while surrounded by killers dressed like royalty.

Across from him sat the Colombian enforcer, Alberto.

Beside him sat The Killer Nun, who's quietly polishing her rosary beads with one hand while stacking chips with the other.

Langichatte glanced around slowly.

Everyone at this table looked like they had buried at least three people personally.

Meanwhile he looked like a Haitian wedding guest who accidentally wandered into organized crime.

He smiled anyway.

"Alright, Lord… let's embarrass evil people professionally."

The dealer distributed the first hand.

Langichatte peeked.

Two of hearts. Five of clubs. Absolute garbage.

He immediately pushed forward $100,000 in chips.

The Colombian enforcer Alberto slowly lifted his eyes.

"You bluff too much."

Langichatte shrugged.

"And yet… here you are nervous."

The flop landed: King of spades. Ten of diamonds. Ace of clubs.

Nothing useful.

Alberto raised aggressively.

The Killer Nun folded immediately without emotion.

Langichatte smiled lazily and doubled the bet.

Alberto stared at him for five long seconds.

Then folded. The room murmured.

Langichatte revealed his terrible hand proudly.

"Faith."

He tapped his chest.

"Haitian superpower."

Alberto looked personally offended by his existence. Now even more upset at himself for not punching LaBond in the face when he had the chance yesterday to do so.

Across the room

ZoGod eliminated two players within twenty minutes.

No theatrics. No conversation.

Just surgical destruction.

Every hand he played felt preplanned by Satan's accountant.

One trembling billionaire shoved all-in against him with a full house.

ZoGod revealed four kings. The man nearly fainted.

Another player accused the dealer of cheating.

Security escorted him away before he finished the sentence.

No one saw him return.

Back at Table One

The Killer Nun finally spoke, after she lost three straight hands.

"You smile too much."

Langichatte nodded.

"Well, my dear, back in Haiti, the1616 Group in Delmas 75 worked very hard to make my teeth look so good. So, I must show them off. Should I give you their phone number?"

The Killer Nun covered her teeth in embarrassment and anger. Then she raised the pot to one million dollars more.

The table stiffened.

Langichatte looked at his cards.

Pair of eights.

Decent. Not amazing. He sighed dramatically.

"Mama didn't raise no coward."

He called. The flop dropped:

Eight. Queen. King.

Langichatte nearly smiled too fast.

The Killer Nun stared at him coldly.

Raised another two million.

Langichatte leaned back casually.

"You know what I love about poker?"

Nobody answered, cause no one cared, but he gave them the answer to his own question anyway.

"You can lie directly to people and still call it strategy."

He shoved all-in. The Killer Nun froze.

The room watched carefully. Thirty seconds passed.

Then… she folded.

The entire table exhaled.

Langichatte scooped the mountain of chips toward himself.

"Arigato."

The killer Nun looked seconds away from ordering a public execution. "I'm Pilipino, not Japanese, you jerk."

Two hours later

Five players had been eliminated.

The overhead voice returned.

"Round One complete."

Hidden walls shifted mechanically.

The fifth poker table now empty began slowly retracting into the floor.

Nineteen survivors now remained.

And the room somehow felt even colder.

ROUND TWO

Four Tables

The new seating arrangement appeared digitally overhead.

Langichatte was now seated directly across from the South African banker.

The man smiled without warmth.

"You play recklessly."

Langichatte nodded.

"You loan money to dictators."

"Fair point." Cards were dealt again.

This time the atmosphere had changed.

Nobody laughed anymore. The stacks were larger. The losses hurt deeper.

Every elimination now felt personal.

The South African banker dominated early.

Massive raises. Brutal pressure. Predatory patience.

Three players folded repeatedly against him.

Then he targeted Langichatte directly.

"All in."

Gasps spread around the table.

Langichatte looked down.

Pair of sevens.

Mediocre. Dangerous. Beautiful.

He stared at the banker calmly.

"You know what my uncle taught me?"

The banker looked annoyed already.

"If a rich man sweats during poker…"

Langichatte smiled.

"that's a definite sign, he's hiding something. I call."

The flop came down: Seven. Ace. Ten.

The banker's confidence cracked slightly.

Turn card: King. River: Seven.

Four of a kind.

The banker revealed his hand slowly.

Straight. Powerful. But not enough.

Langichatte stood dramatically.

"Looks like, My SEVEN NATION ARMY! Overthrows dictators. Next time, make sure you have at least a 720-fico score, with a high CALONEX score before you can even think of challenging me again."

The room erupted with whispers.

The banker slammed the table hard enough to shake chips loose.

Security appeared instantly.

Not for violence. Just proximity.

The banker sat back down quietly.

Three more eliminations followed shortly after.

Now only fourteen players remained.

The walls shifted again. Four tables became three.

ROUND THREE

Three Tables

Now gravity is pulling all the monsters even closer.

Like Scorpion. Niko. The Killer Nun. The African Banker. Alberto. And ZoGod.

For the first time all tournament

ZoGod and LaBond occupied neighboring tables.

Close enough to hear each other. Close enough to study each other.

ZoGod dismantled players methodically. No wasted movement. No wasted speech. Just death by mathematics. Meanwhile Langichatte continued surviving through chaos, instinct, and disrespect for probability.

At one point The Killer Nun leaned toward him quietly.

"You rely too much on luck."

Langichatte smiled.

"No."

He sipped his smoothie.

"I rely on confusion."

The next hand

He won with a bluff so outrageous two players accused him of mind control.

One man folded a flush.

Another folded three kings.

Langichatte revealed a two and a three.

The table stared at him in horror.

"You people think too much."

Hours passed. Bodies disappeared from tables.

Chip stacks grew monstrous. The oxygen in the room itself felt thinner. Then finally, five more eliminations. Only nine players remained. The overhead voice returned again.

"Semi-Final consolidation."

Three tables descended.

Two tables rose.

The second to the final phase had begun.

ROUND FOUR

Two Tables

Now every surviving player could see everyone else clearly.

ZoGod sat motionless beneath the chandelier.

Langichatte sat across the room pretending not to panic internally.

The remaining players:

Langichatte, ZoGod, Scorpion, Niko, The Killer Nun, South African Banker, The Fake European billionaire, A Russian arms trafficker and last but not least The Colombian enforcer Alberto.

Nobody drank anymore. Nobody joked.

Nobody blinked unnecessarily.

The dealer's voice sounded louder now.

"Place your bets." Scorpion fell first.

ZoGod crushed her with a brutal river card.

She stared at him coldly.

"You cheated."

ZoGod smiled slightly. Look at her straight in her eyes.

"Be careful how you talk to me, I cut stingers off for less."

"Forgive me, may your luck continue." Then Security escorted her away.

Next

The Killer Nun lost to Langichatte after he accidentally completed a straight while trying to bluff.

She stared at him.

"You are either blessed…" She stood slowly. "Or deeply cursed."

"Why not both?"

She almost smiled before leaving. Niko lasted another hour.

Then ZoGod destroyed him too.

No celebration. No mercy. Just elimination.

Now, only one table remained. And only four players.

Langichatte. ZoGod. The South African banker. And the Colombian enforcer Alberto.

The Colombian enforcer Alberto died financially first against Langichatte. ZoGod made Ti-Ruby give Langichatte the better hand Just so Alberto could only see red, when he looks at Langichatte.

The banker lasted ten more minutes.

Then Langichatte hit another miracle river card.

The banker collapsed backward into his chair staring at the ceiling like God personally betrayed him.

And suddenly

Everything stopped.

Only two players remained.

Langichatte LaBond. And ZoGod. A 15 minutes recess was giving before they start the final round.

FINAL TABLE

Langichatte LaBond vs. ZoGod

The room changed the moment the final table rose from the floor.

Everything else disappeared into darkness.

The chandeliers dimmed until only one spotlight remained hanging directly above the final table.

Two chairs.

Two men.

Fifty million dollars in chips stacked like miniature skyscrapers between them.

And surrounding the table?

Silence.

Not ordinary silence.

The kind that presses against your skin.

The kind churches and execution chambers share.

Langichatte adjusted his blue tuxedo slowly before sitting down across from ZoGod. His mango smoothie rested beside his chips like emotional support fruit.

ZoGod sat perfectly still.

No smile. No movement. Just eyes. Watching. Calculating. Predatory.

Rose stood behind him in charcoal-black gloves holding a silver case chained to her wrist. Even she looked tense now.

Because this was no longer entertainment.

This was ego.

The overhead voice returned one final time.

"Championship round begins now."

Time: 7:13 PM

It wasn't just the final hand of the round. It felt like the closing scene of a tragedy written by luck, madness, and mango smoothies.

Langichatte LaBond sat at the edge of the final table, swirling his glass like it was filled with aged wisdom instead of fruit and ice.

The crowd applauded… ZoGod gave everyone a stare, immediately the room become silent again.

The kind that presses into your skin like a tight glove. The kind that could break with a single breath.

Langichatte sat under the spotlight at the final table, the green felt between him and ZoGod now more battlefield than game board. There were no more spectators leaning in. No more whispers. Even the air held its breath.

The dealer Ti-Ruby, trying his best to act unshaken and robotic, slid the final two cards face down to each player. The lights above flickered briefly as if even the wiring knew what was about to go down.

Langichatte peeked at his hand:

A ten and a jack of diamonds...

With the dealer feeding ZoGod, his hands. It's going to take a miracle for LaBond to win. He looked up at ZoGod.

The kingpin held his cards with ritual precision. He hadn't glanced at them. Not yet. Just stared at Langichatte with the focus of a man used to dissecting fear like a surgeon dissects a heart.

Langichatte adjusted his sleeves. Licked his lips. Sipped his smoothie.

"Alright, baby. Time to make your ancestors proud. Or confused. Or both."

The flop came down.

 The queen, and the king of diamonds with the nine of clubs.

Still nothing for LaBond, but ZoGod had now all 4 pairs of nines.

ZoGod placed a modest bet with a stack of chips that made a sound like thunder wrapped in silk. The dealer Ti-Ruby barely blinked, but if you look at him close enough, you could tell the pressure was getting to him. All this money, was too much of a responsibility for one man to handle.

Langichatte matched. Casually. He leaned on his elbow and began humming a Haitian folk tune as the turn card was revealed.

Six of clubs.

ZoGod raised.

Langichatte called again without even pretending to do the math. Just pushing his chips in like he was donating to charity.

The river card was dealt:

Ace of diamonds.

But he grinned.

He grinned like a man who had just found the last coconut on an island full of angry monkeys.

Then, slowly, with the kind of grace normally reserved for ballet dancers and dramatic resignations, he pushed his entire stack forward.

(smirking):

"All in."

There was no theatrics to the words. No shouting. Just confidence dipped in absurdity.

A murmur moved through the room like a ripple through oil.

ZoGod tilted his head slightly. Finally, He raised his head and look at his nitwit servant, Ti-Ruby. Like, I know you not that stupid enough to make me lose. So, he glanced at his cards to see what Ti-Ruby gave him to win the game. Four of a kind. "LaBond is bluffing. He's not going to embarrass me again." ZoGod thought to himself.

Then smiled just slightly.

"I called. Four of a kind.

"Please don't tell me you bet 25 million dollars cause you have all four 9s. I'm just messing with you, I have nothing."

ZoGod begin to laugh as he's about to grab all the chips and declare himself the winner. As LaBond shows his hand and continued his soliloquy "Well, I really should have said, I had nothing until the river gave me a Royal Flush. I guess Diamonds are not just women's best friends after all."

The moment the final chip clattered across the felt and into Langichatte's pile, the room seemed to forget how to breathe.

The silence was not empty it was loaded, like a chambered round waiting for a trigger.

ZoGod didn't move, he just couldn't believe it.

Not a twitch. Not a breath. Just stared down at the five community cards as though they had personally insulted his bloodline.

His hands, perfectly still on the felt, slowly curled inward knuckles whitening, veins rising, tendons twitching beneath skin that flushed an ugly crimson. He wasn't embarrassed.

He was offended.

Offended that fate had turned against him and his dealer had let him down.

Langichatte, meanwhile, was the very definition of composed absurdity. He tapped the table twice, gave a warm, humble nod to the dealer, and casually pulled his smoothie from behind a tower of chips.

Langichatte (quietly, to the drink):

"Still cold. Just like this moment."

The dealer, Ti-Ruby right now had an unfortunate resemblance to a puppy caught peeing on a mob boss's shoes, pushed the final stack of winnings across the table with trembling hands. He didn't look up. His eyes were locked on ZoGod's shoes like it had become holy scripture.

His breath hitched as ZoGod's gaze lifted from the table... and settled directly on him.

It was a look that didn't say "You failed me."

It said "Your name is already on a tombstone I'm just deciding the font, cause people like you don't deserve to live."

ZoGod's eyes were fire and venom and winter all at once.

Not rage in motion. Rage in containment and that was worse.

The dealer's hands shook harder. A drop of sweat slid down his temple. His lips moved slightly, like he was praying, but to whom? God didn't answer phone calls from this place.

Langichatte collected the final chips, leaned back, and smiled like a man who'd just finished a particularly spicy bowl of soup.

Then came the words.

Low. Controlled.

Shaped like civility, but dipped in poison.

ZoGod (through gritted teeth) gets up from his seat.

"Congratulations Mr. LaBond. It seems you have best me today."

It wasn't praise. It was a verdict.

Langichatte met his gaze. (smoothly):

"Merci. Always nice to be recognized by royalty."

A moment passed. ZoGod didn't blink. But Rose, standing just behind his right shoulder, took half a step back. With her right index finger, she press the combination code to the on the small briefcase she was holding in her hands.

Without another word, Rose places the bracelet on Langichatte's wrist, with a cashier's check for 25 million dollars. LaBond held his arm like a Shedeur Sanders celebration after a touchdown pass, cause the stone the builders rejected, has become the cornerstone. For those two days of competition, LaBond was legendary. Now Rose couldn't stop herself from gazing at LaBond. While LaBond was too busy celebrating. Showing off his solid gold bracelet, encrusted with diamonds, with a central Z8. Which was meant to represent ZoGod's 8th championship in a row. But now it looks more like ZoGod's embarrassment. And for LaBond, less than a trophy and more like the beginning of a curse cause he had place himself in ZoGod's radar in the worst possible way.

It didn't match his tuxedo. It didn't matter.

He stood. Bowed slightly toward ZoGod.

"I'd say 'good game,' but I don't want to lie twice in one night."

And then without flinching, without rushing he turned and walked away. Behind him, ZoGod remained seated. Still as marble.

But his face? His face had cracked. Not from the loss.

From the insult of being beaten by a joke that refused to stop smiling.

For a full ten seconds after Langichatte walked away from the table, no one moved. Then like a champagne cork finally giving in under pressure the room erupted.

But it wasn't joyful applause.

It was the kind of clapping people do at a funeral when someone shares a story that makes the dead laugh. It was polite, confused, and laced with dread.

Even the applause felt like a performance. One no one wanted to audition for.

Langichatte stood near the velvet curtain, bracelet glinting on his wrist, drink still cold in his hand, wearing a smile that barely covered his nerves.

He turned toward the crowd, gave a modest bow, then adjusted his bow tie like a man preparing to host a game show in a war zone.

Then it came. The voice. Smooth. Crisp. Precise.

A mix between a cruise director and a serial killer's Alexa.

Intercom Voice (Head Auctioneer):

"Now… for my favorite part of this event extravaganza."

A pause. Not long. Just enough to freeze hearts mid-beat.

Head Auctioneer (with glee):

"Attention, everyone may I please have your attention. Please take an hour to freshen-up in your quarters. And after that, I am excited to tell you the after party and more importantly the fundraiser that will help feed the little homeless babies tummies but also their creativity. So please be back here in 1 hour and after that, we will proceed to the Auction Room."

CHAPTER 6
THE AUCTION HOUSE

West Wing, Secret Casino Complex 9:00 PM

The west wing of the casino no longer resembled a place of gambling. It had become a sanctuary of opulence a space that whispered wealth and roared pretense.

Gone were the clattering slot machines, the blur of spinning roulette wheels, and the sharp laughter of lucky (or tipsy) gamblers. In their place stood a venue so polished, so choreographed, it felt like a cathedral where only the devout could afford to sin.

The walls, once covered in mirrored tiles and neon trim, were now wrapped in cream and gold velvet drapery, cascading like waterfalls onto polished marble floors. Hidden speakers played soft Haitian jazz, mingling with the warm, earthy scent of cedarwood and rare incense imported from the mountains of Kenscoff.

Above, a trio of crystal chandeliers swayed gently massive installations shaped like falling blossoms, each petal glittering with hundreds of individual gems. They refracted light over the room like a field of floating diamonds.

Spotlights gently lit the art on display a curated showcase of vibrant Haitian famous paintings, and sculptures masterpieces form the likes of Jean-Michel Basquiat, Marie-Jo Lafontaine, Frankito, Rigaud Benoit, and Jean Claude Damas basically the who's who, in Haitian art. The art was displayed with reverence, guarded by velvet ropes and flanked by fresh orchids in hammered gold vases.

An elegantly dressed server floated by holding a tray of crystalline flutes filled with champagne so rare the bubbles seemed to dance slower than usual.

At the far end of the room, a raised dais had been installed beneath a silk-draped arch where the night's auctioneer would command the room. Behind it, projected onto a massive linen screen, a slideshow displayed images of smiling Haitian children, overlaid with text reading:

"Bid with your heart. Feed with your soul."

– Proceeds directly benefit the Haitian Relief & Cultural Foundation

A string quartet played softly in one corner, their instruments so in tune with the mood it was hard to tell if they were playing or simply breathing in harmony.

The guests arrived in waves of elegance tailored suits, couture gowns, diamonds like stars caught in chandeliers of flesh. They moved through the space like dancers trained in understatement, murmuring in French, Creole, English, and the universal language of wealth.

There was no laughter here. Only muted appreciation. And quiet judgment.

Everything was intentional. Everything was expensive.

And yet beneath the gleam, behind the luxury there lingered a current. Something unspoken. A tension. Because this wasn't just about art. And everyone knew it.

Entrance Archway, Auction House – West Wing 9:15

Langichatte LaBond stepped through the velvet-draped archway with the cautious confidence of a man who wasn't sure if he was entering an auction or accidentally crashing a royal wedding.

(under his breath):

"Cold again? What's with this country? Y'all got central AC but no soul temperature."

He walked slowly, soaking it all in the silk-draped walls, the glimmering art, the people sipping drinks like they cost more than rent. but his attitude remained: equal parts curious tourist, undercover agent, and someone who'd rather be eating griot in the sun.

A passing waiter offered him a salmon roe canape.

Langichatte accepted it and took a bite.

"This is delicious. What is it?"

"Of course it is sir. This is a delectable smoked salmon mousse combine perfectly crisp canape base with pink salmon caviar."

"Wow, so you mean to tell me I'm eating caviar?"

"It would appear so, sir."

"I feel fancy, Thank you Alfred."

The waiter walks away mumbling under his breath "that's not my name you jerk."

People noticed him. How could they not? You would be notice as well if you just won 25 million dollars.

He didn't glide like the other guests. He sauntered. Like a breeze from the islands had snuck into this frostbitten palace of wealth and decided to flirt with everyone's sensibilities.

He passed a group of women in sequined gowns who glanced at him with playful curiosity. One of them nudged another and whispered in French: (quietly):

"Il marche comme s'il prossédait le soleil."

(He walks like he owns the sun.)

Langichatte didn't hear it, but somehow, he felt it and winked in their direction.

Then, just as he was about to admire a bold oil painting of Toussaint Louverture holding a torch in a hurricane, he saw her. Rose.

Standing under a soft spotlight near a series of abstract acrylic works in blue and amber, she looked both regal and untouchable dressed in a white silk gown that hugged her like loyalty, with diamond studs shaped like jagged stars and heels sharp enough to declare war.

She wasn't posing. She just existed beautifully.

Langichatte paused. He adjusted his shirt collar again, checked his breath by breathing into his hand (and immediately regretted it, like he just eaten garlic earlier), then gave himself a tiny slap on the cheek to focus. (to himself):

"Alright, big guy. Let's go put the 'bond' in LaBond."

And with that, he made his way across the room, straight toward the woman who could either be his most dangerous contact or his most thrilling mistake.

Beside the Blue-and-Amber Exhibit

9:23pm

Langichatte approached with a confident saunter, doing his best to appear unaffected by the cold, the glitz, or the statuesque beauty of the woman in front of him. He paused at a respectful distance, studied the painting she was admiring a dramatic piece filled with sharp lines and vibrant blues and spoke just loudly enough for her to hear.

"This one reminds me of the ocean off Jacmel. After a storm, when the sky's still deciding what mood to be in."

Rose turned slightly, raising a perfectly arched eyebrow. Her lips curled not quite a smile, but not disapproval either.

"Poetic. Most people say it looks like a hurricane inside a prism."

Langichatte (grinning):

"I like to think I see beauty where most see warning signs. Probably why I get into so much trouble."

That earned him a chuckle. A real one soft, unexpected.

"You're not like the usual crowd, Mr. LaBond?"

Langichatte (offering his hand):

"I'm just a Haitian export, with international mystery."

Rose (shaking his hand):

"I was really surprised you won. I work logistics and it's true what they say never judge a book by its cover. I guess I owe you my room key, and an amazing and memorable night."

Langichatte (playfully):

"I wouldn't bring it up, but I guess you do on both points. You work Logistics you say? Ah, so you're the one responsible for how dangerously cold it is in here. At first, I question your logic to do so… let's face it, Is this an art auction or a meat locker?"

Rose (smiling now):

"Is it too cold for you Mr. LaBond? I can lower the thermostat just a bit."

"No, it's actually perfect. Seeing you makes me heat up. I wouldn't want my heat to unintentionally destroy these priceless paintings."

She laughed again less guarded this time. She took a sip from her glass, then tilted her head.

"So, Mr. LaBond, what do you do when you're not charming strangers at benefit galas?"

Langichatte placed a hand casually over his heart.

"I run a very modest mango empire in the hills of Haiti. Export trade, eco-sustainable. We only harvest from trees that hum when you sing to them. It's very spiritual."

Rose raised both brows, amused and intrigued.

"Really?"

Langichatte (smiling wider):

"No. I mostly get into situations and try not to die. But I do have an uncle who sells coconut jelly out of a cooler shaped like a whale."

Rose (laughing now):

"Good. I was starting to worry you weren't normal."

They stood in mutual silence for a moment, watching the light bounce off the glass of the framed piece in front of them. The tension between them shifted less playful now. More layered. Something quiet passed in her eyes. Something weighing her down beneath all that polished elegance.

Langichatte noticed. He didn't ask about it. Not yet.

Instead, he leaned closer, just slightly.

"You know, when I walked in here, I thought I was underdressed. Then I saw you, and realized… I'm exactly where I'm supposed to be."

Rose didn't look away.

"You're smooth."

Langichatte:

"I'm Haitian. We're born in rhythm."

That broke the moment just enough. She smiled again, and this time, she held his gaze for a heartbeat longer than before.

"The bidding is about to start, Mr. Mango Empire. Last year we raised over 2 million dollars. This was the most we ever raised in one event in all 16 years of operation. I hope you can help us duplicate what we did last year."

Langichatte:

"If charity is the way to your heart, I will buy the entire building."

She turned and walked away, her heels tapping like punctuation marks on polished marble.

Langichatte watched her go, exhaled slowly, and muttered to himself:

"Okay. She didn't laugh me out of the building. We're winning, baby."

He straightened his jacket, then made his way toward the seating area his nerves dancing, his curiosity growing, and the temperature still entirely too cold for his taste.

Center Stage, West Wing Auction House

The lights dimmed with practiced precision. The hum of conversation faded like the end of an overture. All eyes turned toward the elevated dais at the front of the room.

A spotlight flared to life.

And into that warm golden beam stepped a vision of velvet and pride Swet Holedeuvi, the head auctioneer and self-declared maestro of the night.

He wore a suit so purple it could only have been made by a tailor with a vendetta against subtlety. It shimmered under the lights like oil spilled over satin. His bow tie was a rhinestone constellation. His hair, swept high and back, glistened as if made of secrets and setting spray.

Swet Holedeuvi (beaming):

"Good evening, darlings!"

A polite ripple of applause greeted him.

Swet (arms wide):

"Welcome to our grand auction event! My name is Swet Holedeuvi, and yes yes, sweetheart that is my real name. My mother took one look at me fresh out the womb and said, 'Mmm. This one is going to sparkle.' And sparkle, I did."

Murmured chuckles from the front rows. Langichatte, seated near the middle, sipped his smoothie and whispered:

"Even his voice got sequins."

Swet gestured behind him where a slow-motion slideshow began on the projection screen smiling Haitian children, food drives, families rebuilding homes.

Swet:

"Last year, we raised a record breaking 2.1 million dollars for the Haitian Relief & Cultural Foundation. 2.1. Million. Dollars. Is a lot of money my babies. But I believe it's not an unbreakable record. Those kids need our help, our love, and our support. So, get ready to open your pocket books and buy an art piece or two. Knowing 100% of what we raised is going to a good cause."

Applause now. Stronger.

Swet (pacing):

"Tonight, with your generosity, your glamor, and your scandalously large bank accounts, I know we can do even better.

So get ready to lift those paddles and open those hearts because every brushstroke you buy puts food on a plate, a roof over a head, and art into the soul of Haiti!"

He gave a dramatic bow.

Swet (rising, voice dropping):

"Now. Who's ready to bid fabulously?"

The room warmed with laughter and anticipation. Assistants in black suits fanned out among the guests, holding tablets and whispering protocols.

Rose reappeared, now posted at the edge of the stage, tablet in hand, keeping an eagle eye on the crowd.

Langichatte (to himself):

"First mango smoothies, now bidding wars. What could go wrong?"

He adjusted his bracelet.

And the first painting a breathtaking, modern interpretation of the Haitian Revolution in swirling crimson and gold was wheeled to the front.

Swet (dramatic):

"Lot Number One: 'Fire in the Mango Grove' by Jean-Baptiste Lucien. Starting bid $100,000. Do I hear one hundred?"

A hand rose.

Another. Then ZoGod raise his hand one hundred and fifty thousand dollars. The crowd cheered ZoGod who was staring at Langichatte as if to say, let's play a game and let see who can out bid who?

Swet (thrilled):

"Marvelous! We're off! We're racing!"

Langichatte leaned back, watching, smiling. He gave a gentle nod of the head as if to say I accept your challenge, not knowing just how expensive that moment was about to become.

Swet Holedeuvi commanded the room like a seasoned conductor, directing waves of generosity with dramatic flair and the occasional glittering twirl of his ring-laden hand.

Swet Holedeuvi (grinning):

The next nine lots Langichatte have over bid and bought them for a total sum of 5 million dollars. He became a man addicted to the crowd cheers after every purchase. The more winning bids he won the more Rose was falling in love. And the more ZoGod wanted to kill him.

"And Lot Eleven, titled 'Spirit of Ayiti,' is going once twice SOLD to the mysterious gentleman in the paisley scarf who smells faintly of lavender and vengeance!"

Laughter rippled through the crowd.

Langichatte, had no intention to bid on anymore paintings. But seeing Rose's face showing disappointment cause he didn't attempt to bid on lot 11 gave him all the motivation he needed to re-apply himself to the bidding war.

Or maybe it was the smoothie.

Or Swet's electrifying energy that made every gesture feel like history was being written in sequins.

Whatever it was, when the twelfth and final piece was rolled out a monumental mixed media painting that shimmered like moonlight dancing over Haiti's coast Langichatte sat up straighter.

Swet Holedeuvi (practically purring):

"Lot Twelve, my darlings. 'Heritage: Blood and Salt' by the late Matheus Lafleur. A masterpiece. A journey in pigment. A poem in every line. And since we have already broken our record almost triple time thanks to primarily to Mr. LaBond, we will start this bid at one million. One. Million. Dollars."

A murmur.

A pause.

ZoGod seating in the second row raised his paddle. Until today, he never donated more than ten thousand dollars to any one charity organization per year. But his hatred for LaBond had temporally changed his DNA.

Swet:

"Thank you, darling! We have one million! This is a very good start. Do I hear one point five?"

LaBond raises his paddle.

Swet:

"Yes! Now two? Anyone at two? Anyone at two million?"

ZoGod raised his paddle.

Langichatte looked at Rose determined to impress her. After all, he just won $25,000,000. Giving back a little bit of his winning to a good cause couldn't hurt.

She was standing again near the edge of the stage, observing, lips parted slightly in anticipation. Their eyes met. She gave him a tiny, unreadable smile.

He raised his paddle without thinking.

Swet (elated):

"Two million from our tall drink of tropical water Mr. LaBond! Oh yes, my baby, I see you! I love you. You are so giving, my baby."

The room turned.

Langichatte waved slightly. Smiled, then gave the MJ shrugged. And ZoGod took it all personal.

The bids surged between ZodGod and Langichatte.

Three million. Four. Six.

Langichatte, in a haze of ego, adrenaline, and increasingly aggressive internal pep talks, kept raising his paddle like it was an auction version of cardio.

Swet:

"Eight million, the Mr. LaBond. Do I hear 8.5 million?"

ZoGod raised his hand "Nine million dollars." ZoGod assumed his grand gesture of raising the bid to one million dollars more, will make Langichatte withdraw his paddle. Rose nervously watch LaBond, to see what he will do.

Langichatte blinked. Should he falter from bidding. What's an extra million dollars to a 25-million-dollar man. He raises his paddle and screamed louder than ZoGod "10 million dollars."

Swet (leaning over the podium):

"Ten million from Mr. Langichatte LaBond. Do I hear eleven?"

Silence. But ZoGod is boiling over with anger.

Swet (singing):

"Going once Going twice Going three times, SOLD! To my new favorite person in the world Mr. LaBond."

The room exploded in applause.

Langichatte exhaled.

Then Swet continued.

(grinning wider):

"And let us not forget, ladies and gentlemen, our final bid includes the bonus donation option. As we discussed earlier, the Haiti Cultural Grant Fund allows our highest bidder the privilege to pledge a bonus funds if they so choose for additional contribution to our humanitarian relief!"

Rose politely walked over with a sleek, digital tablet.

Rose acting as Swet Assistant (quietly):

"Would you like to match your winning bid, sir with our standard 10 cents for every dollar?"

Langichatte blinked.

"Match the sorry, what?"

Rose:

"For the charity, my love. It's entirely optional. You can give 5 cents or 10 cents more for every dollar you spent on your last bid. You been so generous thus far, we could skit this part entirely if you like, It's really up to you."

Langichatte looked around. Every eye was on him. Swet. Rose. ZoGod. The cameras. The glowing screen behind him now displaying his name beside the number:

$10,000,000 – Winning Bid

He cleared his throat.

Smiled.

"She called me her love. Wow." Langichatte thought to himself, then loudly spoke:

"Giving 5 or 10 cents more, seems to be too little to give. Make it a dollar more."

Swet gasp. Applause again this time louder. Swet fanned himself with a bidding paddle.

Swet (shouting):

"Twenty million! This man just donated twenty million dollars to the homeless kids of Haiti by buying just one painting! And let's not forget, he had already donated 5 million dollars for 9 other paintings. In one night, my darling LaBond, has donated 25 million dollars. If I wasn't already married to drama, I'd propose to you, right here, right now!"

Langichatte leaned back in his chair. Swallowed his spit. "I did what now?"

Swet gave Langichatte a hug for his $25,000,000 donation. ZoGod seems to recognize that Langichatte didn't seems to want to give his whole porker winnings to charity, and the whole thing amuse him. As Swet ask LaBond to sign over the cashier's check that he won.

"I live in Haiti. I can bring the check to Haiti myself. I won't charge your organization a single cent for the service."

Swet and ZoGod laugh "Mr. LaBond, you're so funny."

"Haiti's champion." ZoGod added.

Rose approached moments later, eyes wide, cheeks flushed.

"That was... extravagant."

"That's me, Mr. Extravagant" LaBond responded with a little sadness in his voice.

Rose (smiling):

"And I thought you were full of hot air."

She leaned in, placed a keycard in his hand, and whispered:

"Room 112. Thirty minutes. I'm going to make you feel like you're listening to Anywhere on repeat."

Langichatte nodded once, too stunned to speak.

Swet Holedeuvi, from the stage, gave him a dramatic bow.

"Ladies and gentlemen, we may have found our patron saint of the evening. Praise be to mangoes and miracles!"

The crowd laughed. The band picked up again.

Langichatte, still smiling on the outside and screaming internally, stood and made his way toward the bar for another smoothie.

Private Suite — Upper Floor of the Casino Resort

Langichatte stood outside the 11 floor, Room 112 with the keycard in hand, heart pounding like a marching band in a steel drum parade.

(to himself, quietly):

"Alright, my brother. Just be cool. You survived a poker tournament; you survived almost donating your pancreas. This is just… conversation. In silk sheets."

He slid the card through the lock. The green light blinked.

Click.

The door opened to a suite so luxurious it could've been rented out by royalty or Famous YouTubers. Dim mood lighting bathed the space in warm tones. The air smelled faintly of orchids and sandalwood. A glass bar glistened in the corner. The bed looked like it came with its own gravity.

Langichatte stepped inside. Hesitated.

Then tried to lean coolly against the doorframe.

The door closed automatically behind him.

Hard.

BAM.

Langichatte jumped like he'd been tased and immediately knocked over a slender end table. A vase full of lilies hit the carpet with a dramatic flop.

"Smooth. Very smooth. Please, relax yourself."

He picked up the vase, placed it back awkwardly, and headed to the minibar. Pouring himself a water, he caught his reflection in a mirror above the sink.

His backward tie was crooked.

He straightened it.

Then crooked it again intentionally. For flair.

Then he approaches the bedroom door

Soft nock. Precise.

He opened the door, and there she was.

Rose.

Dressed not for war this time, but for something quieter, more disarming a silk robe in black with deep red trim, her hair cascading naturally down her back. She wore no jewelry. No heels. Just confidence and eyes that didn't need accessories.

They stood silently for a moment, the charged air between them thicker than champagne foam.

Rose (smiling faintly):

"Still want to impress me?"

Langichatte took a deep breath.

"No. I'd rather just be real now."

Rose stepped inside. She brushed past him, her perfume making his knees reconsider their responsibilities. She sat on the edge of the bed and crossed her legs.

"You really gave twenty-five million to the Haiti fund?"

Langichatte (sitting carefully on the edge of the coffee table):

"Well, yes. Technically. Emotionally? I blacked out somewhere around fifteen."

She laughed. It was a sound he hadn't heard from her before unguarded, free. And then she looked at him, something shifting in her gaze.

"You're not what I expected."

Langichatte (shrugging):

"I get that a lot. Usually right after I crash into something."

She stood slowly, walked over to him, then surprisingly took his hand and led him toward the window.

Outside, the city glittered like scattered stars. Below, the ocean purred against the shore.

"I wasn't supposed to like you."

Langichatte (gently):

"I wasn't supposed to be here."

She turned to him. And kissed him.

Slow. Certain. Not hungry but deep. Like a confession without words.

When they broke, she stayed close, her forehead resting against his.

Rose:

"ZoGod… this operation… it's not just trafficking drugs. It's about infiltration. Corrupting local government. Shipping codes. Blackmail networks. There's a storage compound in Liberty Port hidden under the name Céron Maritime."

Langichatte's eyes widened slightly.

He pulled back just enough to study her expression.

Langichatte:

"Why are you telling me this?"

Rose (whispering):

"Because after tonight, I'd rather be in trouble with ZoGod… than lie to you."

He stared at her. Searched her eyes. Found no deceit. Only fear. And something else. Something genuine.

He nodded slowly.

Then he kissed her again.

And this time, it wasn't just clumsy affection.

It was the beginning of trust.

The room had grown quiet. The intimacy of their kiss had faded into the kind of stillness that comes only after a line has been crossed a shift from performance to vulnerability.

Rose sat beside Langichatte on the edge of the bed, her silk robe now loosely tied, her posture softer than he'd ever seen it. No heels. No makeup armor. No steel in her voice.

Only truth.

She turned toward him, serious now.

"Langichatte… if you're not who you say you are, I need to know now. Because what I'm about to tell you could get both of us killed. I got shot before; the bullet is still on my back. It's not something I want to experience again."

Langichatte didn't flinch.

He didn't smirk.

He didn't joke.

For once, he just nodded.

Langichatte (calmly):

"I'm listening. Please tell me more."

I was supposed to date ZoGod, back then, he was just Jean-Paul Joseph. We lived next door to each other and we were best friends. He respected my mom and my three sisters. My mom really wanted us to get married. He was so sweet, so caring, and so charming. Totally the opposite of what he is now. But I was so afraid to lose our friendship, I never gave him the time of day. Then, he started making money, driving Ferraris and Lamborghinis and women started noticing him. And we became distant to each other. Until one day, I saw him in an afternoon party and he invited me to hang out with him in this Jamaican club the same night. And my mom begs me not to go. She's old fashion. A man must come and take you, not you meeting them in a club at 12 o'clock at night. But me and my best friend Anne, were the leaders to a rebellious ladies' group. So, we went anyway. And a bullet that was meant for ZoGod end up on my back. While I was having surgery, I found out he kiss Anne. And I was never able to really forgive him. To this day every time it rains, I feel uncomfortable cause the bullet is a part of me now. That day, I promise myself never to date a bad boy ever again. I only hangout with him now to connect with people to grow my charitable organization.

Rose stood, eyes tearing… walked to the minibar, and poured two glasses of water. No wine. No games. She handed him one and returned to her seat, clutching hers like it might steady her nerves.

"ZoGod isn't just laundering drug money through fake charities and art. That's the surface. The good optics crime."

She set her glass down.

"He wants to turn Haiti into a wild wild west state. So, the guys with the bigger guns will always win. While he stands at the very top, ruling it all."

Langichatte furrowed his brow.

"Ain't he afraid, with no laws, those same bullets might take him down as well?"

Rose:

"He has secret KKKs, hiding themselves in Canada and Russia. And they are more than happy to give him all the money and support he needs so more of our people can be addicted to drugs."

She walked to a sleek wall console, tapped a code, and a holographic map bloomed into the air Haiti and Florida side by side, dotted with red markers. Ports. Bridges. Checkpoints.

"These are the entry points. Under the name Céron Maritime. But they're just the fronts. The real operations are buried under layers of shell companies and fake charities."

She zoomed in on a location in Port-de-Paix.

"This warehouse here is a conversion site. Military-grade hardware gets re-boxed as farming equipment. Aid shipments are stuffed with fentanyl and smuggled across the water as hurricane relief."

Langichatte's jaw clenched. He said nothing.

Rose turned off the display. The room dimmed again.

"He's preparing something bigger. A regional takeover. Not through war. Through supply chains."

She finally looked at him really looked.

"You're not just here for poker and pretty paintings, are you?"

Langichatte stood slowly, walked to the window, stared out at the glowing shoreline, and said:

"No. I'm here to stop him."

Silence. Then Rose's voice low, serious, loyal.

"Then you'll need more than charm. You'll need everything I've got."

Langichatte turned. Their eyes met. Not as seducer and mark.

But as two people staring down the edge of a storm.

"Good. Because I just donated twenty-five million dollars to this cause. I'd like to get my money's worth."

They both laughed. It was brief. But real.

Rose: "I don't have 25 million dollars to reimburse you, for your donation. But I have something that's priceless and it's my heart and it's yours, if you let me."

"I'll take it, but you still going to owe me $24,999,999."

"Wait are you trying to say my priceless heart is only worth one dollar?"

"Did you hear that come out my mouth?" Rose grabs him. They both laugh and they closed the night with a kiss.

CHAPTER 7
THE MORNING AFTER

Location: Rose's Penthouse Suite – Casino Resort, Room 112 7:15 AM

Langichatte stirred, his eyes blinking open like a reluctant laptop on 2% battery. The Vegas sun, always too damn chipper, spilled across the velvet drapes, casting golden streaks over the champagne-soaked chaos of the penthouse. Designer shoes hung off lampshades. A blackjack dealer's vest was somehow nailed to the wall. And in the corner, a lobster-shaped piñata lay decapitated clearly, the night script went exactly as planned.

He flexed, joints popping like bubble wrap. The sheet slid off, revealing Rose, sprawled beside him like a goddess of mischief wrapped in silk. She opened one eye, smirking like a cat that'd just eaten a $3,000 canary.

"Morning, handsome. How about you make me breakfast?"

Langichatte blinked. Twice. Then turned slowly, dramatically, as if processing the audacity of her sentence required rebooting his entire cultural database.

"I was going to take great offense, 'cause you had the nerve to ask a Haitian man to make you breakfast. That's like asking Mozart to play 'Chopsticks.' But…"

(he glanced down at her with a grin)

"…the coco was fire, baby. So, I'll make you breakfast."

Rose chuckled and pulled him back down for a kiss, the kind of kiss that makes cartoon birds appear overhead and spontaneously combust.

"You better make me breakfast. 'Cause next time we do it, I want to give you all of me."

Langichatte tilted his head, intrigued and now thoroughly awake.

"We had sex last night that wasn't all of you?"

"Boy, please. I only showed you 60% of my skills. That was the demo version. Wait till you unlock the full game."

Langichatte burst into laughter, throwing the covers aside and hopping out of bed like he was auditioning for Magic Mike: Breakfast Edition. He strutted toward the kitchen, almost completely naked except for a sock, boxer briefs and a shoulder holster because you never know when an assassin might pop out of the toaster.

"Guess I'm going to the kitchen to make you breakfast, baby. Hope you like danger with a side of bacon."

"And I'm going to take a shower." As she gets up and disappeared around the corner.

Langichatte strolled into the kitchen like a man on a cooking show where the main ingredient had no regrets and the sponsor felt exhausted from all his night time activities. The space gleamed with opulence sleek granite counters, chrome fixtures, and a fridge that could store both foie gras and family secrets.

Langichatte opened her cabinets to see what ingredients she has for him to work with.

"Alright, let's see what we got. Oh, three types of cereals. Alpen Muesli, that looks delicious." as Langichatte place the first cereal box on the island counter. Then grab the next cereal "Nature's Path Sunrise Crunchy Cinnamon Cereal. You look just as good but I never taste neither one of you." As he places it on the same counter, as he turned back to pick up the third and last box. "Finally, a cereal I know Cheerios. It's delicious and good for heart health.

As he places some soap in his hands, he reached for a bowl to wash before use, a noise behind him shattered the serenity. Not the polite kind of noise. The someone just stepped on a LEGO in complete silence kind of noise.

He turned and froze.

ZoGod's top ninja assassins, the Lee Brothers. Some say they were rejects from the Ozunu Clan. Others say, they come from the 36 Chambers of Death, trained by all nine level masters. The RZA, the GZA, Old Dirty Bastard, Method Man, Raekwon, Ghostface Killah, Inspectah Deck, U-God, and Masta Killa, to be pure killers. Some say they reach the 19th Chambers before they drop out. But none the less, here they were, black-clad, blade-ready, and definitely not here for waffles.

Langichatte: "Seriously? Ninjas? Before breakfast? This is why I don't do Airbnb's."

He through the glass bowl he was holding at the head of one of the ninjas and instinctively reached for the gun tucked in his shoulder holster. Unfortunately, he had soapy hands. The weapon slipped, skidded across the floor like it was late for a rave, and vanished beneath the kitchen island.

The first ninja hit LaBond's chest with his foot. Sending Langichatte hitting and damaging the two door-fridge.

Langichatte snatched a frying pan off the rack like it was Excalibur.

CLANG. Metal met metal as he blocked a katana with non-stick aluminum.

Langichatte: "Oh-ho-ho, somebody's getting a Michelin star in ass-whooping today!"

The second assassin cartwheeled toward him because of course he did sending a foot toward Langichatte's face. He ducked, rolled, and ended up sprawled by the kitchen counter. The gun was tantalizingly close until a ninja punted it further across the marble floor like a satanic soccer ball.

Langichatte: "I hate you. I just want you to know that. Deeply. Viscerally." He reached for the nearest weapon: a rolling pin.

"Alright, Betty Crocker. Let's bake some pain."

He swung. The assassin blocked. Counter-kick. Langichatte flew backwards into the pantry, crashing into a stack of gluten-free sadness and organic regrets. LaBond begins to throw all the plates and other items he could find from the kitchen cabinets.

Dusting himself off, he spotted salvation on the shelf: a bottle of "Rose's Sinister Inferno Hot Sauce – Rated E for Explosive."

Langichatte: "Oh, baby. This is your fault."

He yanked it down, flicked the cap off with his thumb like he was popping champagne, and flung the contents in a spicy arc.

Direct hit. The ninja howled, clutching his eyes, his agony echoing like a banshee at brunch.

Langichatte rolled out, beelined for the gun. One leap. One slide.

Grasp.

He spun around, weapon raised. Breathing hard. Covered in cayenne and glory.

But before he could squeeze the trigger, both ninjas shared a nod like seasoned performers nailing their finale and launched themselves through the shattered kitchen window, vanishing in a flash of black fabric and broken glass.

Langichatte (panting): "Oh good. Now I've got to explain broken windows, blood stains, and a war crime-level hot sauce explosion. This is exactly what Gordon Ramsay meant by kitchen nightmares."

He sighed, dragging himself to his feet as Rose's voice echoed from the bedroom.

"Baby? I'm out of the shower and putting my clothe on. I can't wait to taste your food.

Langichatte stared at the mess. He quickly grabs a bowl and mixes all three cereals as if he was a cereal mixologist.

The sound of broken glass crunching under her bathroom sandals was the first thing Rose registered. Wrapped in a cloud-white towel, steam still rising from her damp skin, she skidded to a halt at the kitchen doorway.

"What the actual fudge?"

She didn't even finish the sentence. Her eyes darted over the wreckage like a casino pit boss on the last night of a losing streak.

The marble counter had a knife embedded in it. The toaster was smoking. The fridge door was open, swinging like a drunk in a windstorm. A ninja mask lay impaled on a spatula. And a very expensive bottle of hot sauce her private reserve was bleeding out across the tiles like a B-movie murder victim.

She looked at Langichatte.

He was bruised. Breathing heavily. One sock on. Holding a cereal bowl with all the casual defiance of a man who'd just wrestled death and had zero intention of explaining himself.

Rose: "How did you manage to do all this damage?"

Langichatte slowly turned to her, surveying the battlefield as if he was the victim here. "Now you know why women don't ask Haitian men to go in their kitchen. You were bound to experience this sooner or later. Anyway…"

(he gestured to the bowl like it was a gourmet offering)

"I made you breakfast. Can't wait to experience the other 40% of your skills. Catch you later."

He leaned in, kissed her cheek, and walked out like he hadn't just turned her five-star kitchen into a deleted scene from John Wick: Master-Chef Edition.

Rose blinked. She looked down at the bowl.

"My special breakfast is cereal?"

She grabs the spoon full and place it in her mouth. Rose (calling after him):

"This cereal doesn't even have milk in it!"

CHAPTER 8
THE STORM BEFORE THE CHILL

Location: Coastal Hideout, Florida Keys 9:00 AM

Langichatte stood atop a weather-beaten dune like a war god in a tailored made blue suit of course the pants are ¾ the length of his legs. The breeze whipped salt into his stubble, the Atlantic hissing below like it knew secrets he didn't. Before him, nestled in the tangle of mangroves, sat the old coastal hideout a battered two-story relic from the Cold War, now hosting its latest round of illegal weapons, whispered deals, and the occasional undercover poker night.

The remnants of a recent storm lingered like a hangover: downed branches, puddles that smelled suspiciously like betrayal, and humidity so thick it could be sliced and served with a mojito. His dress shoes with white socks quelched in wet sand as he descended the dune. This is one of the main locations Rose told him about.

He adjusted the earpiece. Agent Carmichael and Agent Ben are playing back-up babysitters for the day in an un-mark white minivan. Carmichael is on the line.

"I read your report this morning. Speaking only as a concerned friend, I just want to tell you to be careful and slow down a bit. Cause women like Rose will only be interested in guys like you cause they think you have money. And the information she gave you is probably all lies."

"I think I'm a good judge of character. I don't think she was lying to me. She told me this place is one of ZoGod's main hub."

"Don't give her your heart so easy. I think you…"

CRACKLE.

A sudden gust of wind hit like a slap from a weather god with a grudge. His signal disintegrated into a flurry of static and garbled voices. Langichatte winced.

"Come on, not now… hello, hello."

He tapped the earpiece with escalating annoyance. Nothing. It fizzled, sparked, and went radio silent. The wind howled louder, stirring mini whirlwinds that kicked up sand and ghost leaves, obscuring the trail. Visibility dropped. His breath came sharp, chest rising against his tactical vest.

"Great. Wind tunnels. Just what I needed. All we're missing is a mariachi band and a hurricane named Carl."

He trudged forward, instinct overriding frustration. This hideout wasn't marked on any official map.

Halfway through the courtyard, his phone buzzed in his side pocket. It was the kind of buzz that vibrated bone. A warning, not a message.

He checked the screen.

Unknown Number.

He hesitated. Every spy instinct screamed don't answer.

He answered.

A voice rasped across the line, deep and theatrical, like Morgan Freeman if he'd gone fully feral.

ZoGod (voice):

"What do you think you're doing, surveilling my operation? God sees all. I should have known you was a spy for the alphabet boys."

Langichatte froze. The hairs on the back of his neck stood up.

ZoGod (cont'd):

"Since you want to be like Agent Gil so bad, I suggest you go inside the warehouse. I left you a very important clue."

CLICK.

His line went dead. Meanwhile, Carmichael tried again and again to get LaBond on the phone. "Something is wrong. I can feel it in my bones. We need to go and check it out."

Agent Carmichael and Agent Ben grab their guns and speed walk out the minivan.

Cut to: Inside the Hideout – 9:15 AM

Langichatte stormed through the derelict facility, scanning for clues. No electricity. Dust danced in the filtered light. The walls were pocked with bullet holes and the lingering smell of bad decisions.

Then he saw it.

A fresh footprint in the dust smaller than his. New.

He drew his pistol and moved silent, every step a whisper. Room by room, he cleared the hideout until he reached the old comms chamber.

Someone had been here.

A laptop still glowed on the table. The screen showed an aerial view of downtown Miami. A warehouse but what does it mean? Surveillance cameras mapped around it. Tripwire alerts. Infrared sensors. Military-grade motion tech. Someone was planning an ambush or trying very hard to survive one.

Langichatte dug in, downloading the files onto a drive, scanning the data for clues. Names. Routes.

Then the screen blinked.

A feed opened.

Live footage.

Rose.

Bound. Gagged. Bruised but breathing. She sat on a steel chair in a cold room. A shadow loomed behind her. The camera panned just enough to reveal a face.

ZoGod.

Long dreadlocks. With his famous tattoo of himself on his chest riding a dolphin. Eyes that didn't blink so much as calculated. The kind of man who didn't just kill you begged him to, eventually. He gave LaBond a location, in downtown Miami, for them to meet alone. Coordinates. A warehouse. The kind of place where either dirty deals or brutal endings went down.

He stood still for a moment, letting the wind rush over him like a silent witness.

"You want to play hero. Check your phone, you have 12 hours… well technically 11 hours and 30 minutes. Come alone. Or else, you don't want me to explain what or else means, do you?"

Langichatte (muttering):

"Rose… you better still be alive. Or I'm turning this city into a crater."

He pocketed the phone and moved fast. No time to second-guess. No time to call the FBI especially not after ZoGod's warning. "Alphabet shadows." He knew agent Ben and Carmichael were close by. If ZoGod could tap his phone, he could trace the surveillance team. This wasn't just a warning ZoGod will do what he said he will do.

He had less then twelve hours to disappear from their radar.

And in less than twelve hours for him to decide, if he was walking into a trap or a bloodbath.

The screen cut to black.

Langichatte stood frozen. Fury brewed like thunder.

He slipped the drive into his pocket, stood, and whispered:

"You just made the biggest mistake of your life, messing with my Rose. I'm bringing holy water with me to show you, your far from a God."

Agent Carmichael and Agent Ben only found an empty warehouse. La-Bond was no were to be found. By the time they reach inside LaBond was already gone.

Langichatte drove fast. The Charger he commandeered groaned with every twist, engine roaring down the causeway into the heart of the city.

Behind him: no FBI tails. LaBond went off grid. Immediately, agent Arenas' call. "I know what you're planning to do. We need to speak. My office 20 minutes."

"I have no time for that right now."

"Don't make me place your name on the FBI most wanted criminal. That will jeopardize you from saving Rose."

"Ok, I'll come."

FBI Headquarters, Miami – Tactical Division Briefing Room 9:45 AM

Langichatte's dress shoes slammed across the marble floor of the FBI's Miami office like a percussion section on cocaine. The security guards flinched as he stormed through the atrium, waving his ID badge with a grimace that could curdle milk.

Agent Morales (muttering from the front desk):

"Jesus. He's back."

Langichatte didn't break stride.

"Jesus forgives. I don't think I have forgiveness in me to give right now. Where's our director?"

He shoulder-checked the glass doors of the Tactical Division and entered the inner sanctum of federal red tape. Monitors glowed on the walls heat maps, satellite feeds, algorithmic threat levels. In the center stood the alpha himself: Director Gil Arenas, head of the Miami division.

Langichatte stormed into the briefing room like a grenade with legs. Agent Arenas looked up from a holographic projection of downtown Miami. Two agents near him instinctively stepped back.

Agent Arenas (gruff):

"Langichatte. You know I can put you on the shelf for going off-grid. Surveillance says you ditched your car then highjack a private American citizens car by impersonating an FBI agent. Do you have anything to say in your defense?"

Langichatte

"I don't have time to play with all your American rules. Like Franky, I'm going to do it my way now. He kidnap Rose."

Agent Arenas:

"You're jeopardizing a classified operation."

Langichatte:

"No, I'm going to burn his whole operation down to the ground. ZoGod called me. Threatening to kill Rose. Sent me an address. Said no shadows, or she dies."

Agent Arenas's jaw tightened.

"We are not letting you walk into that death trap alone."

Langichatte stepped closer, lowering his voice until it was sharp enough to cut glass.

"He's watching. If I show up with heat, she's gone. You think I'm about to let Rose get ghosted on account of bureaucratic paranoia? Hell no. There's forty percent more of her I still need to get to know."

That got a chuckle from agent Ben. Agent Arenas's glare shut it down instantly. Agent Carmichael really wanted to say something but Langichatte's frustration kept her quiet.

"You want to be a hero, fine. But you don't get to make that call solo. This isn't a vigilante gig. You work under our badge now."

Langichatte crossed his arms, eyes blazing.

"I work under survival, sir. And right now, Rose's running out of it."

Agent Arenas:

"If you're dying to die early, we've got a fast-track training program that'll make your coffin more patriotic. You don't walk into enemy territory without tactical clearance. I'm not greenlighting anything until you complete it."

Langichatte blinked.

"Training? As in a desk orientation and a 'how not to cry in a shootout' PowerPoint?"

Agent Arenas:

"Wrong. The Accelerated Operator Readiness Pathway – AORP."

Langichatte snorted.

"Sounds like a terrible boy band."

Agent Arenas:

"It's a 4-hour tactical proving ground. We call it Hell's Hallway. You complete it, I'll consider your request. Until then, you're not cleared to operate within fifty feet of that warehouse."

LaBond visibly upset.

"4 hours. Ain't nobody has time to waste like that. Rose is in trouble; I need to save her."

Agent Arenas

"Listen here LaBond. This is not Haiti. You don't get to do whatever you want to do when you want to do it. This here is the US mother-father A, and over here, we follow protocols. In case you didn't realize it, that's one the reasons our country is so great. Pass our test and you'll a double 0 license. Then you can kill all the bad guys you want, with impunity."

Langichatte sighed, cracking his neck.

"Great. Just what I needed: government-sanctioned CrossFit with bullets. Okay, I'll play your game. Bring it on."

Quantico was less a training facility and more a crucible an imposing fortress carved out of iron will and centuries-old discipline, set under skies so relentlessly gray they looked like they'd been dipped in cold steel. The sprawling brick buildings, with their dark, weathered facades, rose like stoic sentinels, watching over the maze of firing

ranges, obstacle courses, and classrooms where futures were forged or shattered. Towering watchtowers lined the perimeter, their surveillance cameras sweeping methodically over the grounds like unblinking eyes, a constant reminder that here, the line between order and chaos was etched in gunpowder, sweat, and the bitter bite of coffee. Only the elite of elites get to call this place home.

Langichatte LaBond stepped off the black-ops helicopter, the rotors chopping the air with a deafening roar, stirring the dust and tension hanging thick over the compound. He moved with the casual swagger of a man who had survived storms far worse than this and had grown impervious to the sterile, militarized tension that gripped every inch of Quantico. His duffle bag hung loosely from one shoulder, his aviator sunglasses reflected the cold steel of the watchtowers, and his jaw was clenched not from aggression or determination, but out of sheer frustration. The helicopter coffee had betrayed him yet again, tasting like burnt regret mixed with crushed ambitions.

Before he could adjust his gear or catch a breath, a clipboard-wielding instructor approached, his expression a blend of suspicion and impatience.

Instructor Hill:

"Agent LaBond, welcome to Tampa. You must have powerful people behind you, for you to be place last minute on my roster."

Langichatte didn't miss a beat. His grin was quick, effortless.

"I prefer 'legend in progress. I don't have time to waist, can we get started with this test, please."

Hill's jaw tightened into a grunt that could have been agreement or just irritation. He gestured toward a massive steel-reinforced door at the end of a concrete corridor. Above it, a sign was stamped in cold, official letters:

"Accelerated Operator Readiness Pathway – AORP"

Hill pushed the door open with a metallic screech that echoed down the hall. Inside was a stark, industrial arena that looked like a hybrid between a gym, a shooting gallery, and a high-tech playground for tactical nightmares. The floor was padded with thick steel mats, targets blinked with electronic precision, vehicles lined up ready for rapid deployment, and a crystal-clear pool shimmered under harsh fluorescent lights. Instructors clad in black tactical gear stood like statues around the perimeter, their eyes scanning everything with the precision of hawks who had seen too many disasters to tolerate nonsense.

Hill nodded toward a large digital board flickering to life on the far wall.

"Four modules. One hour each. Fail one, you're out."

Langichatte raised an eyebrow, smirking.

"If I ace all four, do I get a decoder ring and a hug?"

Hill's face didn't crack, but there was a twitch in the corner of his mouth that suggested Langichatte's humor might just be tolerated barely.

"Better. You get a ticket back to the real world. Or permanent desk duty. Your call."

Langichatte rolled his shoulders, dropped his bag with a thud, and cracked his knuckles. The faint hum of the building's air circulation mixed with distant gunfire and the rhythmic slap of trainers hitting mats. This was the arena where reputations were forged or crushed.

Training Module 1: Hand-to-Hand Combat

The gym was a living, breathing entity of sweat, iron, and silent judgment. The stale air hung heavy with the mingled scents of overworked muscles and old rivalry. Walls lined with mirrors reflected the tense faces of recruits, while mats stained with years of scuffed attempts and bruised egos served as the battlefield for the day.

Langichatte stepped into the center of the mat, the focus of every gaze. The fluorescent lights overhead buzzed faintly, casting a clinical glow over the room, but in that moment, everything else faded. Opposite him stood Calhoun a man built like a human vending machine. Broad shoulders, thick arms rippling with muscle, and a grin that promised pain. Calhoun was an ex-Marine, a man who had clawed his way through more battles than most could count, and who now proudly declared himself the "God of Grapples." (grinning):

"I heard you got beat up by a girl, last time you did this test. You must be a total embarrassment to your parents. Hope you've updated your will, rookie."

Langichatte's eyes sparkled with mischief as he slowly, deliberately unbuckled his belt, letting it fall in a lazy loop.

"Actually, my mother has four kids, 2 girls, 2 boys but I'm my mom's favorite child. You see, in my country, men don't hit women. So, it was a culture shock for me when I had to fight a female agent. Yes, she beat me, but I didn't even try to fight her back. But you... I'm going to have fun fighting you."

Calhoun (eyebrows knitting in confusion):

"Since, you already removed your belt, I think you should surrender your booty, so I can take it easy on you? I think it's the best strategy you got. With me by your side, no bad guy will ever threaten you ever again. I guarantee it, cupcake."

Langichatte chuckled softly.

"Why don't you come and get it."

With a sharp flick of his wrist, the leather belt snapped through the air with a crisp crack, slicing a clean arc like a whip. The sudden sound made several recruits jump.

Calhoun, predictably aggressive, lunged forward with the raw force of a charging bull, aiming to overwhelm by sheer power.

But Langichatte was no stranger to unpredictability.

With effortless grace, he sidestepped, his movements fluid like water slipping between rocks. In one smooth motion, he wrapped the belt around Calhoun's wrist mid-swing, the leather curling like a serpent striking its prey. The sudden resistance caught Calhoun off guard.

Langichatte's hands twisted sharply an expert maneuver born from countless bar fights in Caribbean ports and narrow alleyways where quick thinking was survival.

With a powerful flip, Calhoun was thrown clean over Langichatte's shoulder, crashing onto the mat with a resounding thud.

The entire gym fell silent.

All eyes fixed on Langichatte, who straddled Calhoun's chest with the relaxed confidence of a man who had just delivered a masterclass.

"That's a TKO. But don't worry, if I ever date you. You'll never have to worry about anyone ever embarrassing you like that ever again. But sadly, you're not my type."

Calhoun groaned, the fight draining out of him in defeat.

The instructor standing nearby, Hill, scratched notes onto his clipboard, his face unreadable but nodding grimly.

"He hurt Papa Bear. I should get in the ring and fight him."

The room remained charged with a mix of awe and disbelief. Langichatte's unorthodox style had just rewritten the rules.

Recruits exchanged glances some impressed, some wary. One whispered to another, "Did he just turn a belt into a weapon?"

Langichatte, standing tall, offered a cocky grin.

"Sometimes, you gotta get creative when the odds aren't in your favor."

The hand-to-hand combat module had just found its most unconventional champion.

Training Module 2: Shooting Accuracy

The shooting range was a sanctuary of silence. Walls layered with ballistic insulation muted even the sharpest echoes. Targets hung at fixed intervals, distant specters waiting to be judged by lead and intent. It smelled of gun oil and cold metal, the air sterile almost too clean, like no story dared to stay long in this place.

Langichatte stepped onto the firing lane with deliberate calm. His boots clicked against the polished concrete floor like punctuation marks. The overhead lights hummed above him, casting long shadows across the black-and-gray partitions. Other recruits had come and gone from this booth some proud, some embarrassed, all humbled. But now it belonged to him.

The instructor, a rigid former Delta Force sniper named Mercer, stood off to the side. Square-jawed, unreadable, the kind of man who probably measured his emotions in ballistics and blood type. He handed Langichatte a customized Barrett MRAD. Custom grips with matte black finish.

"Your target's the silhouette in red. Distance: 1500 yards. Three rounds. You miss; you fail."

Langichatte took the Barrett

"Wait 1,500 yards that's 4,500 feet away.

Instructor Mercer

"Yes, it is. But you could always quit. Save us both the aggravation of your whining."

LaBond didn't speak right away. He stared downrange, where the silhouette waited a faceless figure marked for judgment.

Then he closed his eyes.

The sterile range faded.

In his mind, the red silhouette twisted, reshaped itself. It became a man. Not just any man ZoGod. Dreadlocks swaying like serpents. A gold tooth that glinted when he lied. Eyes that never blinked when he gave an order. A voice that could curdle kindness.

And then Rose. Bright-eyed, sharp-tongued, always three steps ahead of him, even when she teased. The laugh that echoed through their stolen night and a love from a fraction of one second, that became unbreakable. The way she'd dared him to believe in something real.

She'd trusted him. Believed in him. And now she was gone.

Langichatte (softly, almost inaudible):

"This one's for her."

He opened his eyes. Steady. Sharp.

BAM.

The recoil was smooth controlled.

BAM.

The second shot followed a heartbeat later, as precise as the first.

BAM.

The third hit with the finality of a sentence ending in blood.

The red silhouette jerked slightly from the impact. On the digital screen beside the lane, the target zoomed in, revealing all three shots clustered in the exact same hole. A bullseye with no room left to breathe.

Dead center.

A stillness settled over the range. Even the nearby recruits stopped their own drills to glance over.

Instructor Mercer lowered his clipboard. His mouth twitched slightly an expression somewhere between a smirk and reluctant respect. It was the first movement his face had made all day.

"No one can ever appreciate it more, than the person who's begging for it."

Langichatte didn't look back. He walked off with quiet confidence, placing the sniper weapon down gently on the table. Not tossed, not slammed just left, like a message.

A single nod to Mercer. No smugness. No bravado.

Then he kept walking, coat swinging, shoulders square, as if the ghosts in his head had been momentarily satisfied.

Behind him, one of the younger recruits whispered: (awe-struck):

"Did he even aim?"

Mercer muttered under his breath:

"He aimed with something none of you have yet. Pain."

Langichatte disappeared into the hallway, leaving behind nothing but the sound of the target retracting, and a silence thick with recalibration.

Training Module 3: Defensive Driving

The training yard was a symphony of organized danger. Dust hung in the air like fog made of failure. Cones marked out cruel turns. Concrete barricades loomed. Mannequins dressed as civilians and criminals popped up at random intervals. Tires smoked. Engines roared. Somewhere in the background, an instructor's clipboard snapped in half like a broken dream.

Langichatte surveyed the scene like a man about to improvise a ballet with horsepower.

At the far end of the lot, a lineup of vehicles waited like bored soldiers. A tactical black SUV gleamed with reinforced panels and a center of gravity that said "military budget." Next to it: a turbocharged Mustang that looked like it moonlighted in street races. Both were popular picks among the recruits.

But Langichatte?

He squinted… and pointed past them.

Langichatte (grinning):

"That one."

Covered in a fine layer of disuse and political memory sat a faded green Jeep, boxy and stubborn. Its paint was peeling. Its tires sagged like they'd seen things. A raccoon had clearly nested in the backseat and left a receipt.

The instructor squinted at the clipboard

"That thing hasn't moved since Bush was in office."

Langichatte (with conviction):

"Perfect. No one sees it coming."

The instructor

"Cadet, you understand you're racing five professional racers. If you don't get to the finishing line first, that's an automatic fail. Do you understand? And are you sure that's the car you want to drive?

LaBond

"Yes sir, I understand and yes, that's the car I want to drive."

He hopped in. The driver's door screeched. The ignition clicked, coughed, gave up, then rallied with a reluctant roar like a smoker waking up for court. The Jeep rattled to life, protesting every second.

The timer beeped.

Recruits peeled out in waves, screeching through lane-marked obstacle tracks with mechanical grace.

Langichatte?

He floored it and immediately veered left.

Not just off-course. Way off-course.

He plowed through a line of orange cones like he was bowling for chaos. The Jeep's suspension screamed. Langichatte whooped.

Instructor (into his radio):

"Uh… he's off the grid. Where is he going?"

Observer (watching drone feed):

"I… I think he just took the raccoon trail."

Langichatte barreled into a wooded thicket rarely used since the legendary "Possum Incident of 2017." Branches whipped across the windshield. Mud flew up in gobs. He spotted a sharp curve and drifted around it badly, but successfully.

He punched the horn. It played half a note and died.

Then he jumped a dirt mound like a man auditioning for a movie no one funded. The Jeep caught air for three heroic, physics-defying seconds, then slammed into the ground, shedding a hubcap like a badge of honor.

Ahead loomed an old storage shed, barely standing.

Langichatte didn't slow. (to the Jeep):

"You hold together, I'll drive us home."

He smashed through the wooden wall. Dust, broken shelves, and a forgotten Christmas wreath exploded into the air. For one breathless second, nothing moved. Then the Jeep emerged on the other side filthy, dented, but alive.

As he rounded the last curve, the other recruits were still navigating a hairpin turn designed to simulate "urban panic."

Langichatte didn't even blink.

He skidded sideways across the finish line in a shower of gravel and rooster-tailed mud, laughing like someone who had just broken a curse.

The Jeep wheezed and promptly died in a victorious slump.

Langichatte (stepping out, coated in filth, glowing):

"Alternate routes. Highly underrated."

The instructors stood in silence. One of them clapped. Just once.

Another recruit whispered to his friend: (shaken):

"Who is this guy... and where did he come from?"

Instructor Hill scribbled furiously on his notepad. The words were barely legible beneath the grease smudge from the drone crash, but three words stood out: (muttering):

"Unpredictable. Unteachable. Unstoppable."

Langichatte tossed the Jeep keys to no one in particular and walked away, leaving behind a cloud of dust, a ruined shed, and a legend but the racing community would deny this race ever happened.

Training Module 4: Swimming

The Olympic pool shimmered like a slab of polished ice under fluorescent lights. Its surface was mirror-smooth, still and smug, reflecting the harsh ceiling like it was daring someone to disturb its perfection. Chlorine hung heavy in the air, the scent sharp, clinical a poor imitation of the sea.

Langichatte stood at the edge of the pool as if confronting a generational enemy.

He stared into the deep end; arms folded tightly over his chest. To the casual observer, he looked calm stoic, even. But inside, Langichatte's nerves vibrated like struck piano wire.

Cold water and he had an understanding. A cold truce forged in years of tropical blood and inherited mistrust. Cold water didn't want him. He didn't want it. The end.

Instructor (dryly):

"We heard you can't stand cold water. So, we made sure our water temperature was perfectly heated at 50 ° F. you need to do twenty laps within 6 to 9 minutes to pass our Elite Competitive Swimmers Test. No floaties. No drama. There's no shame for you to go back home."

Langichatte didn't move.

He looked at the water.

And in that still, blue pain he envisions Rose as a ghost.

In this painful daydream on a rooftop pool in Miami.

He saw her mouth gagged, her hands bound, her eyes wide. He saw ZoGod grinning, sharklike, as he vanished into the night. He remembered the blood, curling through water like ink in milk.

Langichatte blinked.

The scene shifted.

Petite Goave. Haiti. Age eight.

Turquoise waves tickled the white sand. His uncle Fanfan's fishing boat bobbed offshore. Mango trees danced in the wind behind his house. His grand-mother, radiant in a yellow dress, called from the porch:

Mami Ché (laughing):

"Langichatte! Come eat before your turkey tasso gets cold!"

With his favorite side, of sweet banann peze. Back then there was no avocado, or coconut, or olive oil, everything was fried in regular oil. Salt kissed the air. He remembered running barefoot down the path, skin warm with sun, joy humming through his limbs. He remembered diving into the sea not because he had to but because he could.

Back then, water was a playground.

Langichatte's jaw tightened. He exhaled once. Sharply.

"Cold or not. Water is water, and you mastered that the same time you learned how to walk."

Then he dove in. Stroke. Stroke. Turn. Glide.

No splash. No wasted motion. He sliced through the water like a man remembering himself. Each stroke was, a reclamation of nuclear fusion. LaBond met the frigid resistance with a heat that came from his curated memories. Sixteen past relationships catalogued in his chest, five of them true, incandescent loves. Though four more hunted him, like his best friend sister. He kept those poems as draft, unwritten confessions he'd never dared performed, though they should have been uttered. When life handed him lemons, his strange superpower is to go to his top five. The women who'd given him his happiest, brightest, most scored moments but he chose to only remember their warmth

With each lap, his past fell behind him.

Lap 3: He remembers the sexy big girl he had a crush on. Her named is Amber. And she looks like a younger Halle Berry to him. She gave him so many cute names and he was so naïve and happy. But Jade her cousin, always played the hater.

Lap 7: The chase. Her name was Linda. She was from Canada. She was the woman he wanted to marry. In fact, she said no to him 4 times. He may make it sound like a joke if you ask him, but the first time she said no to him… he cried like a baby.

Lap 12: The gunshot under moonlight Was his ex-wife. But since 2015, he never opened his mouth to speak her name out loud, now he only referred to her as his stepson's baby mother. Cause outside his father, she was the most loving and painful experience he ever had with another human being. But his love for his step-son never died.

Lap 18: His semi-final breath was Rhe. The 4th woman he had ever loved in his life, but she was nuclear fusion from the sun itself. But when she was happy, her excitement was contagious. When she decides to dress up, he doesn't look at her in her eyes. His willpower is not that strong.

Lap 20: Redemption. Is the fifth and last woman he had fall in love with. Her picture is on the cover of Threefold Desire. She thought him to love without regret. He just met Rose. And he will do anything, to not make her a memory.

He touched the wall with both hands. Surfaced. Gasped. 5 minutes 45seconds.

He pulled himself out with quiet dignity, water sheeting off his back like he was rising from baptism. (panting):

"That… wasn't so bad."

The instructor approached with a clipboard in one hand and a towel in the other, eyes wide behind dark lenses. (murmuring, stunned):

"You beat the academy record. By 7 seconds."

Langichatte took the towel and ran it across his face, his breath slowing.

"I was motivated by spite and nostalgia. Deadly combination."

Another recruit, still clinging to lane 6 like a drowned cat, coughed violently.

(in disbelief):

"Was that even human?"

Langichatte didn't answer. He walked away dripping, shoulders square, towel draped over his neck like a cape. Behind him, the pool rippled in his wake like a memory slowly fading back into calm.

The instructor jotted something down:

Langichatte LaBond – his unorthadox, and yes, the spelling is right. His exactly like that light skin underground rapper. But his not light skin and his not a rapper. But just like the rapper, they're both, undiscovered diamonds.

Post-Training Briefing – 2:45 PM

Back in the operations room, instructor Hill, reviewing LaBond's scores with Director Gil on his phone.

"Technically, he passed Sir. Trust me, we did everything we could to make him quit. But like my favorite underground rapper Unorthadox and my favorite single from him. His about that Action."

Agent Arenas:

"This guy is about to fight 101 dogs by himself. Not dalmatians. The street kind. If we let him go there, there's no doubt about it, his going to die."

Hill:

"I hate to admitted but agent LaBond is special sir. He beat-up my boyfriend, shot 3 bull's-eye, four thousand five hundred feet away. Ran through the obstacle course with an old school Jeep and still beat professional drivers by 45 seconds and broke the 20 laps record by 7 seconds in frigid water. I'm telling you; I wouldn't believe it if I didn't witness it myself. I wouldn't bet against him."

Agent Arenas

"Wait, LaBond beat-up Papa Bear?"

Hill:

"Please, when you see him don't crack no jokes about that. Papa Bear is very sensitive, I know how you get. Don't forget I got dirt on you too."

Agent Arenas

"Look, send my guy back to Echo-9. And agent Hill don't ever threat me again. There's a reason why your just an instructor and I'm a director. I have way more dirt on you then you have on me. By the way, did you ever told Papa Bear you're the mask instructor that beat him and cause him to never get his double 0 license and go on the field. True be told, he was never Papa Bear. His more like Baby Bear, and mama bear never wanted him to play outside with real bears, with real fangs and real claws. Cause they eat little bunnies for breakfast cause they know how to use the weapons nature gave them. Hahahahaha"

Agent Hill quickly hung up the phone, look around as if his boyfriend could overhear his conversation.

Locker Room – 3:00 PM

Langichatte dried off, and put back his blue suit. Agent Hill sent him back to Echo-9 on the same helicopter that brought him here. It's a 30-minute flight. As he got on the helicopter, he took no joy to look at the scenery all he kept doing is reflect.

"Alright, big guy. She's waiting. Time to be the hurricane."

He checks his phone and looks at Rose's last message:

"My love, I'm under my bed. I believe I'm about to be taken cause there's four men with guns in my condo right now. I hope you have special skills like that Irish guy. And before you get confuse, it's not the UFC one it's the other one. They grab me, my love. Wait, let me tell my baby one more thing. When you barbecue them, bring Haitian hot sauce."

Langichatte smiled.

He tucked a bottle of her favorite brand into his belt:

"Baby, I'm bringing fire."

Back to Echo-9 — 3:30 PM

At the Helicopter pad, agent Ben and Agent Carmichael were already there ready to greet LaBond.

"Look LaBond, I'm sorry. You pass the AORP test, you should be a double 0 right now but Agent Arenas our director and the entire higher up in our organization has some apprehensions about you. They don't think your 1st round 1st pick, they're thinking more like 5th round 144th pick. Our intelligence told us that there's about one hundred killers not including ZoGod inside that warehouse. They don't believe you could play with the big boys. They think, if you go out there too soon, you're going to get killed."

"Honestly, it's been my calling to be a hero since age 6. So, I only have two choices now. Go there, save Rose and get arrested for being a vigilante. Or go there and die trying. Either way, I'm going there like I'm 50… when he raps about robbing the industry, cause none of you can stop me to be the man, I know I am."

"I normally keep my opinions to myself, but our Director Agent Arenas is right. This is a suicide mission. What makes her life more important than yours. I'm sure you could find creamier, if you could just stop looking behind you. Trying to save a chick who had to know, she was working for a bad guy. Her hands are not that clean."

"Agent Carmichael, I have to try to save her. If ever somebody would kidnap you, I would do everything in my power to save you too."

"Really, you would want to save me?" "Yes, absolutely."

"Look, agent Arenas wants you to play in one last pre game to test to see how fast you can think on your feet. You pass it then for sure, for sure you get your double 0 license. Save your Rose. Heck, you may even get a shoe deal from Nike. 009 Haitian Pride."

"Look, Agent Ben, I don't know you really and you don't know me. Just like you'll never know me the way I know me and I will never know you the way you know you. This has to be the last test, don't try to play me. Ain't nobody got time for that. So, what do I have to do?"

The doors to Echo-9 training facility creaked open like the entrance to a gothic opera. Fluorescent lights flickered above padded walls, turrets, and booby traps. Rubber bullets. Stun drones. Electrified floor panels. It was less of a training space and more of a sadistic playground.

Langichatte was handed a GoPro helmet and a fake weapon. He waved the gun around with a sigh.

"You guys are compensating for something, right?"

Agent Ben (smirking):

"Just survive. That's the only goal. If you can reach the end without tripping an alert, Agent Arenas will sign off."

Langichatte:

"Copy that." BEEP.

The door slammed behind him.

Instantly, a motion sensor turret activated and fired a barrage of bean bags.

Langichatte ducked, rolled, and swore in Creole.

"Agent Arenas, you passive-aggressive donkey! I really don't have time to play these games. I need to go save my Rose."

He sprinted forward, ducking behind foam cover, then leapt over a tripwire rigged with paint mines. Two drones whizzed by, scanning for heat signatures.

Langichatte dropped flat, pressed a hand to his chest, and slowed his breathing.

"Okay. Just pretend you're dead inside. Like a DMV clerk."

The drones hovered. Passed. Moved on.

Langichatte rolled forward, took out a simulated guard using a chokehold taught in a Port-au-Prince back alley, and slipped into the next corridor.

A holographic hostage screamed.

System Voice:

"Scenario: Rescuing Civilian Hostage Under Hostile Fire."

Langichatte looked around. Two fake terrorists. Sniper sensor above. One flashbang prop on the ground.

Langichatte smirked:

"Time to improvise."

He grabbed a broken pipe, wrapped it in the hostage's shirt, and threw it toward the far wall.

The sniper fired. Missed. Langichatte lunged in the opposite direction, dropped the fake guards with two calculated hits, and yanked the hostage free.

Langichatte:

"You're welcome, imaginary Karen. Someone should really write a book to tell your life's story."

System Voice:

"Scenario complete."

The final door opened. Langichatte stepped into the exit chamber, chest heaving.

Agent Arenas stood waiting. (slow clap):

"Not bad. Only took you... 37 minutes."

Langichatte:

"I took a detour. Your training room was missing sarcasm."

Agent Arenas tossed him a black duffle bag.

"You've got tactical clearance now LaBond. You are the first Haiti/US double 0 agent. In conjunction with the Haitian government, your license will be recognized by both governments.

Langichatte zipped the bag. And saw a special combat dress shoes and a wallet with his obsidian-black FBI badge with a bold "009" laser-etched into the bottom.

"that's a big letdown, that's all I get in my gift bag."

He turned to leave.

Agent Arenas called after him.

"That's not all, agent Ben is going to bring you to the situation room. Dr. Wolf is going to hook you up with more toys."

Agent Ben after bringing agent LaBond in front of the door of the situation room to meet Dr. Wolf. Decided to give LaBond a peptalk.

"Hey, by the way, you got this. Your about to fight one hundred and one professional killers. Your exact dilemma reminds me when I had to fight this one guy. He was so intimidating it felt like I was fighting one hundred and one bad guys. I was fighting to stay in a circle and he was fighting me to get me out of some imaginary circle. But in the end (as agent Ben used his right hand to tap on his wedding ring finger) I became the circle."

"Wait, are you trying to compare the fact I'm about to fight one hundred and one villains to save my girlfriend to a time I imagine, you were begging your father-in-law for you to marry his daughter?"

Agent Ben:

"Well since you put it that way, I can see where they maybe discrepancies between both stories. Trust me, you don't want to meet my father-in-law, he's the equivalent of one hundred gangsters, plus one."

Langichatte look at agent Ben and thought to himself. "White people logic, sometimes… is really different, but let me inquire more."

"How did you know she was the one and what's your wife's name?"

"From the first time I lay eyes on her, I knew, there's something about her. And oh yeah, her name is Marie."

"Buy Marie some flowers today, and tell her you love her. And don't take the time you have with her for granted." After making that statement, agent LaBond opened the door and walk in the room, leaving agent Ben to ponder what he just told him.

4:00 PM

Inside the Situation Room, the air was different thick with something heavier than humidity: anticipation.

Special Agent Dr. Wolf: As his eyes caught Agent LaBond entered the room. He immediately began to search for a special box.

"Agent 009. Just the man I was waiting for. You are now the first Haitian with a double 0 license, and because of that fact all future Haitian agents will share the code last name LaBond. Haiti and U.S. Government's most charming, most questionable, and most unpredictable asset." Just as he found the box he was looking for. He place it in between him and LaBond on the table, then opened the complex compartment that locks it in place.

A sleek matte-black sidearm sat nestled inside, fitted with biometric sensors along the grip.

Special Agent wolf:

"This here my dear friend is your personal firearm. SIG Sauer P320, fingerprint-locked to you. Custom suppressor. Auto-recoil dampening. And smart targeting if you decide to shoot from the hip while saying something ridiculous."

Langichatte picked it up, the gun purring softly as it scanned his fingerprint and unlocked.

"Ooooh, baby talks. I love when they purr. Okay, I'm loving what door number 1 just gave me. Do I get more doors?"

"This wouldn't be the situation room if you didn't get more gifts."

"Okay, Wayne Brady. Let's make a deal. What's behind door number 2?"

"I'm glad you ask. How about a custom made Richmenlooks suit hand delivered from Atlanta, GA. But not just any Richmenlooks suit. A bullet-proof one of one. Custom-cut to your (as he gave a slight cough to clear his throat cause LaBond insist his pants must always be 3 quarters the length of his legs. As Dr. Wolf continue to finish his statement.) questionable proportions. Lined with military-grade nano-weave. Fireproof, blade-resistant, shock-absorbing, and insult-proof up to a point."

Langichatte (grinning):

"How about ex-girlfriend-proof? Her sexy legs hunt my dreams so much. No matter what I'm dreaming about, she'll appear then strutting all around, trying her best to win a talent show, but there's no show. And when I wake up, I have to eat 4 mangos, just to control the hunger inside me."

Special Agent Dr. Wolf:

"Sounds like only therapy can help you with that problem. But I do have a special bulletproof belt for you to wear with your suit. With a custom belt buckle 009."

"You have nothing that can protect my heart but, but the belt, the gun, and the suit will give me a fighting chance to protect my life."

Lastly, Dr. Wolf placed three small orbs on the table. 2 of them are slightly bigger than the last one and they all glowed faint blue.

"Smart mini bombs. Voice activated. GPS-tracking, and wall-penetrating."

Langichatte:

"What's the blast radius?"

As agent Arenas entered the room, heard LaBond's question and decided to answer it himself:

"The 2 dark blue ones, are two big badaboom. And the smaller light blue one is a niniboom. You can throw these booms at anything. And they will transform whatever it hit, into the fifth element. Guaranteed. They. Will. Protect. You."

Langichatte leaned back, whistling low.

"You folks sure know how to make a man feel loved."

Agent Arenas (serious now):

"You're going into this alone. No backup. No air support. No cavalry. You're outnumbered, outgunned, and out of your mind."

Langichatte (deadpan):

"Just the way I like it."

"Maybe, the last toy I give you can balance your fortune a bit."

As agent Arenas reached into his coat pocket and tossed him something with a sharp jingle.

Langichatte caught it midair keys.

He turned them over and saw the glint of silver lettering etched on a black key fob: C8 CORVETTE. LICENSE PLATE: USA009.

Langichatte (gasping dramatically):

"Oh. Oh baby, where you been all my life. I got to say, outside of Haiti. USA is the closest thing to heaven money can buy."

Agent Arenas:

"This is not a regular C8 corvette. This one comes with the Night-Rider package."

C8 corvette: (female voice)

"Agent LaBond, my primary function is to protect you. I have six missiles and a machine gun that could shoot a thousand round of 50 caliber bullets in just 5 minutes. I'm here for you, my baby."

"We design her to be a soldier's perfect companion. What you say, what you press, is what she does. Zero lag, zero talk back, twin-turbo V8, Hyper car killer, 1064 horsepower. This is technology excellence."

"Sorry, for the first time in my life, I'm at a lost for word. I'm having my first visual orgasm."

Langichatte took no time to fully suited up. Place his badge on his belt, holstered the SIG as he places his C8 Corvette keys in his pants pocket. As he stands in front of his new car inside an opened door elevator. Agent Arenas walks up to him and pop Langichatte's shirt collar.

"there's nothing more we can do for you now. You just got pimp, FBI special force edition. My money's on you to win. Now go out there and get your baby back."

As the doors closed behind him, the nearby junior agents resumed their tasks quiet, tense, still watching him with an odd mix of admiration and disbelief.

Agent Ben, turned to Agent Arenas.

"Sir… why did you tell him; your money is on him to win? You bet me one thousand dollars; he doesn't reach the 6th floor alive."

Agent Arenas didn't look away from the elevator display as the numbers ascending.

"Well, let me ask you something, agent Ben. With all your training, all your clearance, your perfect test scores from The Cathedral School of St. John the Divine, would you take on this mission by yourself?"

Agent Ben (stammering):

"Absolutely I would, why don't nobody ever believe me when I tell them… my father-in-law, really is one hundred and one Purple Cobras."

Agent Arenas finally turned, meeting his gaze with eyes carved from stone.

"Agent LaBond is one of us now. So, in my heart, I would love for him to win. But my brain tells me, that man has a better chance to become the president of the United States, then reaching the 4th to 5th floor. But hear me clearly son, I may think his delusional, but he has all my respect… cause he's still going. But when he dies, you better get ready to pay me my money. Cause you just as delusional as him, nobody is buying your story that your father-in-law will make you bleed your own blood. That man is seventy plus years old. one hundred and one purple cobras in one man. Boy please.

Your father-in-law barely has the strength of a garden snake. So please stop repeating it."

Agent Ben: "So, if you don't believe in my story and you don't believe him, I guess you got a backup plan?"

Agent Arenas: "We have a 300 Spartans team circling that warehouse. On their smart phones, watching everything we see. Faraway from detection, but not too far away, where they can't detect. One word from me or if they see agent Langichatte falls, my team of Avengers, will do, what we do best…and avenge him."

Agent Carmichael gave agent Ben one thousand dollars.

"Put me in for one thousand dollars too, LaBond is more a lover than a fighter. I wish he wanted more for himself like a woman with good credit, and good family values. than running after a suicide mission or if he survives, those types he's running after, will only give him pure debt."

Agent Ben "I get the white girl betting against the black man, cause white girls are notorious to secretly attack black men. Specially the rich ones. But you four are black, betting with a white man for the downfall of another black man. You'll should be ashamed of yourselves. I'm telling you, I survive my father-in-law, his going to survive this."

Agent Arenas turned to agent Ben:

"Every time I hear your father-in-law story, you make me see the error of my ways. Put me down for another thousand. God knows my heart; I don't want a black man to fail, but the odds are too good to pass up on this bet. So, son, in my Fat Joe voice, again your delusional."

Agent Arenas (quietly):

"Good luck, Agent 009. I wouldn't mind losing these two thousand dollars. Even though, the payout pays double."

CHAPTER 9
SEVEN FLOORS TO HELL

(or: how one man, one car, and zero common sense took on a private army)

Int. FBI underground garage elevator dusk

The elevator hummed upward. Inside it, agent 009 Langichatte Labond sat in a jet-black C8 corvette like a man who had made peace with death and then sent death a strongly-worded rejection letter.

The leather seat hugged him like it already knew this was goodbye. The custom HUD glowed to life. He adjusted his cufflinks, cracked his neck, and looked exactly as cool as a man heading toward a one-percent survival probability had any right to look.

C8 corvette: "Just so you know agent 009, my new baby. I have completed your mission briefing. And I'm so sorry to say, your estimated survival probability is 0.78%. Would you like me to enable the funeral playlist?"

Labond: "No. Play Dajé I Can Be."

C8 corvette: "Noted. I'll play your little happy go lucky song for you, but time like this my baby, demands you to listen more miracle songs. Statistically speaking, if you switched to kirk franklin and Yolanda Adams, divine intervention would boost your odds by 2%. I've taken the liberty of pre-loading a gospel mix. It includes God favored me. Seems relevant."

Labond: "Play what I asked. And for the record, didn they tell me, you don't talk back."

C8 corvette: "Boy please, you already sign the contract saying you're my new baby and you belong to me. I told you already I'm gonna play your catchy little song then immediately after that, you are gonna hear my gospel play mix. I said what I said. Period."

The elevator doors opened. The corvette rolled out under a single spotlight, sleek and predatory, its twin exhausts humming like a threat not yet delivered.

Two floors below, in the *FBI situation room, Agent Gil Arenas watched the feed. His expression didn't move. But his eyes did. They were afraid.*

✦ ✦ ✦

Ext. Miami docks moving dusk

The black C8 Corvette sliced through Miami's golden hour like sin on wheels. LaBond gripped the wheel, sunglasses on, suit immaculate one of one, Richmenlooks bulletproof, because if you're going to possibly die, you may as well die in something the police can't afford.

C8 ai: "Agent 009 my new baby. I just realize, I may lose you on the same day I just got you. Why even attempt this? What we're about to attempt isn't a mission. It's a suicide note written in motor oil."

Labond: "I know. What choice do I have?"

C8 ai: "Don't be a fool, you have several excellent ones, in fact. For starters: Did you know Rose has a co-leader. Her name is Anne. She's a lieutenant, right here in Florida. Accomplished, and beautiful by all accounts. I've pulled her file."

A photo of Anne appeared on the dashboard screen. The C8 let it linger there. Professionally.

C8 ai: "She's licensed to carry, great taste in footwear, and critically she has never once been held hostage in a seven-story warehouse full of mercenaries. I'm just saying. You could download Domino Gwaan Bad on your phone. Have a lovely evening. And get to know her instead."

LaBond: "You are right, she's drop dead gorgeous. But… I met Rose first. I can only play with the cards I have in my hands."

C8 ai: "My last owner used to love to save people. He was so good, we lasted 4 seasons. Until he realizes, he can't save them all. He's a lifeguard now in Venice Beach. Just watching the waves, living his best life. We never broke up, he just left me with a dear John letter. I wish I knew, was there ever a day or Knight, did he ever wake up, reaching out for me."

Labondwith tears in his eyes: "I can't worry about tomorrow, if I'm afraid to live for today. This Canadian woman ask me one time, why do Haitian men say I love you so fast? I told her, we just know what we know. And what we don't know can't carry a bigger value in our lives. I know the difference between a mango and an orange. It's one thing to see a person and pick her to be your mango but will she pick you to be hers?"

C8 ai: "I get it. Just know, we may not all get the story book ending we all dream of. But know, I'll ride with you till the end."

The corvette surged. Miami blurred behind them. The mission was on.

✦ ✦ ✦

Ext. Miami docks ZoGod's warehouse 5:45 pm

The abandoned warehouse loomed at the edge of the docks like a bad idea that had committed to itself seven stories of rusted steel and criminal ambition, squatting beside the Atlantic as if the ocean owed it rent. The sun was setting, which felt symbolic. The sun clearly wanted no part of what was about to happen.

LaBond stepped out of the corvette slowly, like a man attending his own execution with a fresh haircut. Then his phone rang.

ZoGod: "(smooth, theatrical) Welcome dear friend, to your last day on earth. That's a nice car, LaBond. After you die, I'm sending it to Haiti. So, my people can understand nou pa eguaray. We're not stupid over here."

LaBond: "I'm here. Now release Rose."

184

ZoGod: "Oh, nonono Mr. LaBond. That's not how the game is going to go, my friend. You're not Danny Roman. If you want Rose? You must come inside and get her yourself my boy."

LaBond studied the warehouse. Two football fields long. Seven floors of steel and shadow. No visible doors, no windows at ground level. The C8 completed its scan in three seconds.

LaBond: "ZoGod wants to be as big as Walmart."

C8 ai: "Correction: this looks more like Amazon prime architecture. They'd have your coffin delivered before you even ordered it."

LaBond: "He's hiding the front entrance. Clever."

C8 ai: "Please. I don't need doors. I make my own. Permission to redecorate?"

LaBond: "Permission granted, make it big. I want to walk in with style."

The hood panel slid open. A shadow missile armed itself with a sound like a polite clearing of the throat before a catastrophic announcement.

Boom. The steel wall disintegrated into a jaw of jagged metal and smoke. When the dust cleared, the entrance was wide enough to drive through which was the point, because the C8 drove through it.

LaBond stepped out. Brushed a fleck of ash from his lapel. Looked at the hole. *"God, I love America."*

ZoGod's voice rolled in from hidden speakers, filling the cavernous first floor like a villain who had definitely rehearsed this.

ZoGod: "(amplified) Yes, yes, yes, welcome, Mr. LaBond. I knew you were going to make this game very special to me. I see your using a loophole under our agreement. You did come alone, but you stroll into my fortress with a living car that shoots missiles. Do you call that fair? I don't know. But you still a dead man walking."

LaBond: "I call that, having a personal card dealer. But she won't make the mistakes Ti-Ruby did. You fake Elnohim, I want to bet you another 25 million dollars, you can't cheat death. You down."

He patted the corvette's hood.

LaBond: "Jesus only took 3 days to rise back up. How many days you think you'll need?"

C8 ai: "(headlights flashing) Slow it down, like Conceited my baby just diss you, El. No. him. My baby is so clever."

ZoGod: "Ok I'm game. Your exotic car killer is Hilarious, let's see how far your car's jokes get you. Seven floors. Each one a maze. One hundred hired killers spread across them. You survive you find me on the seventh floor. With your precious Rose. Or "

A pause. Soft, almost kind.

ZoGod: "Put a bullet in your brain now and I let her go. My word is better than most Gods."

LaBond checked his gear. Fingerprint-locked sig Sauer. Mini bombs in the inside pocket. Smart-watch tracking his vitals. He looked up at the warehouse ceiling, then delivered the line with the calm of a man who had already done the math and decided math was someone else's problem. *"Seven floors. Maze full of mercenaries. Feels like someone watched die hard backwards and added trauma. Yippee-ki-yay, you false divinity. I'm coming for you."*

And the warehouse swallowed him whole.

✦   ✦   ✦

Floor one: ex-military

Int. Warehouse floor one continuous

The first floor was a cathedral of crates steel and shadow stacked two stories high, alleys winding through them like streets in a city designed specifically to get you killed. LaBond's footsteps echoed. The silence was the expensive kind: curated, deliberate, ominous.

C8 ai: "(earpiece) Twelve men. Automatic rifles. Military formation. You've walked into a shark tank."

LaBond: "Then let's see if Mister Wonderful can offer a good deal."

The floodlights snapped on. And there they were. Twelve mercenaries in black tactical gear, rifles raised, balaclavas pulled low, advancing in textbook staggered formation. Their leader's voice was clipped and professional.

Merc leader: "Spread wide. Pin him down. Send this wanna-be alphabet boy back to Haiti in a casket."

LaBond: "Twelve to one. I feel underdressed."

C8 ai: "Correction, twelve to two. I'm not just here to drive you wild, I'm gonna make them blow their gaskets."

They opened fire.

The warehouse became a percussion concert with worse ticket availability. Muzzle flashes strobed in the dark. LaBond dove sideways, sliding behind a steel crate as rounds chewed holes through it sparks, shards, concrete dust, the general ambiance of a bad Tuesday.

He leaned out, fired four precise shots. Two mercenaries went down shoulder and leg each, alive and very annoyed. He ducked back. A few rounds answered him from three different directions.

Then three mercenaries flanked from behind and unloaded twelve shots directly into his body.

LaBond: "(hitting the floor dramatically) I'm dead. I'm dying. Lord help me, please "

He rolled. Patted himself. Checked his chest. No holes. He looked up at the three confused mercenaries. They looked down at him. A shared moment of professional confusion.

LaBond: "Wow. I'm not dying. I'm like Batman, but less known. I'm Blankman."

Merc #1: "shoot him in the head."

LaBond broke cover in a low sprint, Haitian street-fighting instincts doing the driving. He zigzagged between crates, firing clean shots, moving like a man whose body had made a deal with physics that regular people weren't privy to.

He reached the nearest enemy. The mercenary swung his rifle. LaBond shoved the muzzle sideways, drove his elbow into the man's throat, and ended the conversation with a brutal efficiency that made the word "neck-snap" feel inadequate.

He used the falling body as cover, fired over its shoulder. A third attacker came from the flank. LaBond dropped the pistol, caught the rifle mid-swing, delivered a knee that rearranged the man's ribs, then put him to sleep with the gun handle.

LaBond: "I feel like Goldberg, Who's next?"

From the far end of the floor, the remaining mercenaries regrouped and tightened their lines. Two had catwalk positions. LaBond slid behind another crate as bullets shredded the air above him. He took a bad turn and now his cornered.

"Mother, Father… I got a little too cocky with myself, C8 help.

C8 ai: "Delighted to help, my baby. Time for me to redecorate."

The C8's panels slid open. Twin turrets unfolded with a sound like the future arriving ahead of schedule.

Two hundred rounds in sixty seconds. The turrets spoke in .50-caliber poetry. Crates exploded. The catwalk operatives took gravity personally. When the sound finally stopped, the smoke was thick enough to taste.

LaBond: "Wow, I love what you did with the place."

C8 ai: "I know right. We should definitely think about opening an interior decoration firm together."

The mercenary leader raised his rifle. Aimed for LaBond's temple. Fired. LaBond moved but not fast enough.

The corvette jumped. Actually, jumped like its tires were made from Air Jordans with a point to prove. The bullet pinged off the bulletproof glass into harmless sparks.

C8 ai: "I'm not keeping score but it's only the first floor and you owe me your life twice over. Black Car Magic."

LaBond, from the floor, spotted a knife nearby. Scooped it. Threw it in one fluid motion. The blade spun end-over-end and buried itself somewhere the mercenary leader would not soon forget. The man's scream reached a frequency previously undocumented by science.

The remaining mercs hesitated. That heartbeat of hesitation was all Langichatte needed.

He surged. Grabbed the fallen rifle. It roared. He rolled, yanked a mercenary by the leg, slammed him into the ground. Three jaw-cracking punches, two leg shots. The last two tried to retreat. LaBond chased. Tackled both. Slammed their heads together with a sound like two bowling balls meeting their destinies. Silence.

The gunfire stopped. Smoke curled upward. Twelve mercenaries lay distributed across the floor like a particularly grim modern art installation.

LaBond stood at the center of it, chest heaving, blood on his knuckles. The corvette's headlights swept across the carnage with the energy of a proud parent at a school play.

C8 ai: "Not bad for a man without airbags. You almost got your skull ventilated back there. You owe me big."

LaBond: "Fine. Next car wash is on me."

C8 ai: "Just a car wash? Please, Sir, I could do that for myself. You need to give me a full-body detail. New tires. New windshield. New everything. You better treat me like a queen if you want me to drive you wild. That's why I'm here, to get your life together."

LaBond: "No one gets a sports car expecting to have a quiet engine. But note, you can't be my queen, if I'm not your king."

From the ceiling, ZoGod's voice returned. Colder now. Less amused. "It's only the first floor, and I'm already hearing trouble in paradise. Hahaha. Please, I beg you to leave this place. You are walking in the wrong direction Mr. LaBond. My mom always said soft heads needs harder lessons. The next floor is going to split yours open. I've hired the second most powerful gang leader from Haiti. His name is Grill Master."

Labond: "(smirk, tilting toward ceiling) Looks like my 4th of July party is gonna come early, fine by me. Just please tell your men to aim better. I hate when people waste ammo."

C8 ai: "And I hate when people underestimate me. Nobody touches my new man. Not on my watch."

ZoGod: "It's your funeral."

✦　✦　✦

Floor two: the ambush

Int. Warehouse floor two ramp moments later

The iron stairs groaned under LaBond's boots. Smoke from the first floor clung to him like a souvenir. The C8 followed on the spiral ramp, head-lights cutting arcs through the gloom.

C8 ai: "(low) Quick FBI search: Grill Master is Barbecue's younger brother. His gang the Bistronegs are straight-up killers."

LaBond: "They sound like they need to open an eatery. Sell avocado toast. Poor Haitians had that figured out years ago. I'm ready for whatever barbecue party they want to start."

C8 ai: "Baby. Is rose really worth all of this?"

LaBond: "I'll let you know after she gives me the other forty percent."

C8 ai: "(disgusted pause) Men. So small-minded."

The second floor was darker. Floodlights flickering. Crates stacked into narrow corridors like a city of bad intentions.

LaBond stepped in, pistol raised. Instincts screaming: wrong. Too quiet. Too clean.

Then came the clicks. A dozen rifles chambering at once.

From every corner, shadow became men. Twelve Bistronegs emerged with the quiet confidence of people who'd been paid in advance and planned to stay that way.

ZoGod: "(speaker, smug) Welcome to the second floor Mr. LaBond. I see you have a few minor booboos. I'm sure it's nothing for us to worry about cause you tough right. Remember I tried to save you, I told you don't go to the 2nd floor. We have set up a surprise end of January 4th of July, end of life party in your honor. Now, its too late for you to turn back. Grill master, barbecue this burger with no cheese for me."

The Bistronegs started shooting on sight.

Labond: "Twelve again. I'm starting to think ZoGod can't count higher."

The C8's voice ripped through his earpiece like a fire alarm.

C8 ai: "Michael hit the floor now."

Labond: "Who the hell are you calling Michael?"

C8 ai: "Sorry, my new baby. Old habits die hard. But, floor. Now."

LaBond dropped flat. Face first on the steel. No hesitation.

The turrets unfolded with the sound of destiny setting up its equipment.

C8 ai: "Say hello to your dream car, dream car, gentlemen."

Three hundred rounds in ninety seconds. Apocalyptic. The sound rattled the walls, made the air tremble, and permanently reclassified several of the Bistronegs' career ambitions. Several of them was screaming like 5-year-old-little-girls.

One of the Bistronegs yelled above the carnage:

Bistroneg #1: "Grill Master! You told me I'd get a free flight to America and a hundred US dollars to help kill one Haitian man. You never said the Haitian man in question was Haitian Rambo. Mercy for the free flight, mwen p ap mouri jodi a (I'm not dying today). My sister Dominique is a nurse in Fort Lauderdale. I'm out."

He was out. Several of his colleagues, upon hearing the terms and conditions suddenly laid bare, felt the same spiritual calling and followed behind him toward the nearest exit which happened to be a window.

One of the remaining Bistroneg, furious, wheeled on Grill Master:

Bistroneg #2 : "Ou pa bou moune! You gave them a free flight and a hundred dollars. But you made me pay you two goats to be here. Until I die, I will never forget this."

He dropped to the floor and played dead with the commitment of a method actor three days before oscar nominations.

Others followed. Eyes shut. Hands folded. Sincere prayers murmured to God in Haitian creole.

Meanwhile, LaBond crawled across the floor as sparks skittered inches from his face, a ricochet grazing his ear, hot blood spraying his cheek.

LaBond: "(grunting) next time warn me about friendly fire "

C8 ai: "(smug) you're still breathing, aren't you? You're welcome."

The storm settled. Smoke layered the air in grey curtains. Most of the Bistronegs were down. A few true believers still crawled toward their rifles. And from somewhere near the window Grill Master stood scared, water ran down his face. His hands shook. His entire philosophy of violence was undergoing a live revision.

ZoGod: "Where you think you're going. We had a deal. You told me anything Barbecue could do; you can do better. He's just one man.

Grill Master: "I'm sorry bon fré. I should have never left Haiti. Back home, when I pull a gun on a Haitian, they pray to Marie or Jezi. First time I pull a gun on a Haitian in America and he shoots back. I can't give you a refund on the 300k you put down for my services, cause that goes against my company policy. But I promise you, if this man goes back to Haiti, I'm going to make my big brother Koupe tét li (cut his head)! Gratis, free"

LaBond rose from his crawl, bruised and bloodied, and stalked through the haze like something the smoke was afraid to follow. Walking towards Grill Master "How about you do it now?" Grill Master scream and jumped out the window into the ocean below, his voice trailing back up:

"(fading, wet) Don't step foot an Haiti. Gade kijan ou neg fé m pipi sou mwen, the day I see you in Haiti, I ma make you, pipi on yourself too!"

LaBond incapacitated the remaining true believers with surgical precision shoulder, leg, the dignified minimum.

Then came the sneeze. From one of the "dead."

LaBond: "Get up. Or I shoot."

Bistroneg #3: "Please I've heard of you, Langichatte LaBond. All the good things you do in Haiti. You're a hero to all of us. Even bad guys like me. Let me live and get back to my daughter Shelldina Petit-Frère. She's a dance choreographer founded the Shann Academy of Dance. I don't want her without a father. We all want to see Haiti change. I pray you're the spark that actually does it."

LaBond tilted his head left. The ex-Bistroneg got up, walked to the window, and jumped into the ocean.

Bistroneg #3: "(splashing, distant) Merci, Langichatte!"

Silence, broken only by dripping water and the quiet dignity of an ex-mercenary with a newfound political opinion.

C8 ai: "see? Easy. Just follow my instructions and you won't die. I'm basically GPS for violence."

LaBond: "GPS doesn't usually involve body parts on the floor."

C8 ai: "Depends on which neighborhood of St. Louis, Missouri you're navigating into."

In the FBI surveillance van, four agents watched the feed with the intensity of people who had accidentally created a hit reality show.

Agent Ben: "(grinning, stacking cash) Told y'all. My brother got this. Floor number two cleared."

Agent Arenas: "(throwing money on the table) I hope you right. 2 down, 5 more to go."

Agent Carmichael: "(arms folded, smiling) LaBond improvises. Always has. Also, can I tell you all a secret, he's starting to turn me on."

Agent Arenas: "Girl please. You know we all are FBI agents in here right. We're the ones who normally take the case files with no clues, to find the clues. You drop so much bread crumbs out here Stevie Wonder himself would find it, and make a remix for you to Usher's song You Got it bad. So, please, we all know you have a thing for them Zoes. Tell us something we don't know."

Agent Ben step closer to Agent Carmichael "Did you know, sometime around WW11, my great grandmother gave birth to my grandfather in Haiti, which make me 15% Zoe. That's why Marie loves me so much. It's true what they say about us. So, I get why your so addicted to people like us."

Agent Carmichael gave Agent Ben a look and went and sat down next to Agent Arenas. Arenas shook his head and said:

"This guy, every time he opens his mouth."

ZoGod's speaker crackled. His voice had shed the smug and was now wearing something sharper. "Damn your car. Those damn bullets flying everywhere. If you think you're going to fight massa like Nas. Remember, massa still had himself a hanging tonight. So, keep letting your car do your killing. Just know, that's not skill. That's cowardice."

LaBond: "If being a cowardice gets the job done; I'll take it."

C8 ai: "Cowardice? I am state-of-the-art murder on wheels. Put some respect on my rims."

ZoGod: "The third floor will carve you apart. Let's see how your car fares in protecting you against blades instead of bullets. I'm going to make you feel like you're remixing Syl Johnson's voice like the Wu did in Hollow Bones."

LaBond: "Then sharpen them well."

✦ ✦ ✦

Floor three: the ninjas

Int. Warehouse floor three continuous

The third floor had prepared a whole aesthetic. Lanterns flickered along the walls. Incense coiled through the rafters. Wooden crates arranged like shrines. The salty tang of the sea mixed with something older and more theatrical.

Then steel hissed.

Twelve figures in black shinobi shōzoku uniform appeared from the smoke silent, precise, blades catching the lantern light in cold, beautiful flashes. Ninjas. Actual imported ninjas.

ZoGod: "(triumphant) Do you like my guests? Straight from Japan. Each trained for ten years in mountains and silence. They promise me, they will make one thousand slices on your body before you die. And I'm gonna be here for every slice. UFC has nothing on this. Yeah Boy. Flavor Flav."

LaBond: "(unimpressed) You flew ninjas to Miami? That's not a crime. That's tourism." As they entered floor number 3, the C8 Corvette got caught in a fish net trap cleverly hidden. Now dangling in the air by a hydraulic machine, all she can do now is watch.

ZoGod: "Oh oh! looks like your number 1 weapon is now just a spectator. What are you gonna do now my boy. You can't have a farewell tour, if they don't love you like you think they do. Call me Mr. Four-time NBA world champion Draymond Green baby."

C8 ai: "Save yourself my baby, I'll be ok."

ZoGod: "No, he won't be. Attack."

One darted forward, blade slicing downward. LaBond snapped his belt free from his waist in one smooth motion the leather cracking like a whip across the attacker's wrist. The katana hit the floor. LaBond looped the belt around the man's throat, yanked, drove a knee into his jaw. Bone cracked.

The others surged. The belt became a weapon, whip, snare, and strangler simultaneously. LaBond used crates as cover, walls as springboards, six centuries of fashion history as a combat instrument.

C8 ai: "Okay my baby, I see you. Netflix dojo fight in 4k. You're the Haitian Bruce Lee with fashion accessories. You're doing good, you got this."

Six ninjas down within minutes. Then the seventh moved. Differently. Calm. Low. Precise.

He stopped, studying LaBond's form with something like recognition.

Ninja #7: "where did you learn this Shotokan karate style?"

LaBond: "(slight smile) You notice it. You're smarter than the rest. So, spare me a few moment, so I can recite my monologue. You see, a long time ago, a man by the name of Master Teruyuki Okazaki came to Haiti to teach Japanese at my school Saint-Louis de Gonzague. He saw three kids try to jump me. I didn't back down. It was the first time I really used my belt the way my father used to use his on me when I misbehaved. My wild swing style made Master Okazaki took a shine to me. He could never teach me Japanese. The language beat up my tongue quite a bit. But he taught me Shotokan and I quickly became his number 1 student. Our relationship grew to father and son. He was the greatest thing that happened to me."

Ninja #7: "Is this for real? I can't believe my ears. What a surprise coincidence. I was also taught by the legendary master Teruyuki Okazaki. And I believe... I was his number one student."

A beat. Then the seventh ninja removed his mask. I am Master Hiroshi.

Hiroshi: "I must be transparent. We share the same father. The same master. But you must impress me before I call you brother. You five remaining ninjas, do not interfere with this fight."

Katana vs. Bulletproof belt. The duel was extraordinary precise against improvised, Japanese discipline against Haitian street-forged instinct. Hiroshi neutralized everything LaBond threw. LaBond countered everything Hiroshi brought. Like looking into a mirror that had trained in a different country.

Without a word exchanged, both men knew: master Okazaki had two number-one students.

They were about to bow when the six unconscious ninjas woke up, assessed the situation, and chose violence. The other five followed suit. Seeing how skillful Langichatte was with his belt. They target it, and slice it in four pieces. With his primary weapon gone the ninjas begin to focus on offense. LaBond fought with nothing but grit and fury. He drops 2 of the ninjas with a headbutt, elbows, and knees. But the katanas, they kept slicing him up. LaBond suit though now fully shredded stop a lot of body parts from being separated from his body. Blood caught the lantern light.

C8 ai: "(frantic) Baby, you're leaking. Stop leaking. You are not a juice box."

Hiroshi had seen enough. He plunged back into the fight not against LaBond, but beside him. Stopping a killing blow meant for LaBond's spine.

LaBond: "Why are you helping me?"

Hiroshi: "Those other ninjas are not students of Master Okazaki. So, they are no brother of mine. Go save your Rose. I'll handle the remaining eight."

ZoGod's voice sliced through the speakers.

"Hiroshi, what are you doing? Don't bother coming to my office for your paycheck. I'll also be calling my credit card company to cancel the flight I booked you. Good luck explaining that to ice how you got in America with no paperwork. Five million dollars to the first ninja who brings me Hiroshi's head."

The remaining ninjas gripped their katanas. Surrounded Hiroshi. He didn't look worried. He looked like a man who had trained for this moment in a mountain somewhere and was overdue.

Hiroshi: "(to LaBond, absolute certainty) Go. Now. Brother. I've got this."

LaBond hesitated one second, press the red button on the hydraulic and release the C8 from its detention. Then, they went.

ZoGod: "(to LaBond) Boy you got lucky there. Look at you. Bleeding all over. Every cut cost me a fortune in delivery fees. Forget Rose. Save yourself while you can. Reach that fourth floor and I guarantee you a penthouse suite on the upper room. Do not pass go. Do not collect two hundred dollars."

LaBond: "Sounds good to me. I'm coming to give you, my deposit."

ZoGod at a loss for words turned to Rose. "You sure you only gave this man just 60 percent of your skills. This man is possess.

In the FBI van, the agents lost professional composure entirely.

Agent Carmichael: "(quietly, to herself) If you're doing all this just for some cheap chocolate. What would you do for my Klondike bar."

Agent Arenas pick up a walkie-talkie: "I don't think this man is going to survive another floor. Get ready my A-Team. When I say go, I want everybody lock and loaded."

Agent Ben: "(stacking more cash) Agent Arenas, I know you're the director and all, but I pity you if you think you're going to win this bet."

Agent Arenas: "I hope you right, I love your confidence in him."

✦ ✦ ✦

Floor four: the women assassins

Int. Warehouse floor four continuous

LaBond climbed the stairs trailing blood like a map of everywhere he'd been in the last twenty minutes. His shirt was shredded. His chest gleamed. The C8 followed on the ramp, engine dropping to a quiet, worried rumble.

C8 ai: "(muttering) Three floors down and you look like high-end hamburger meat."

LaBond: "(grinning through blood) Hamburger tastes better when it's spicy."

C8 ai: "If spicy is the new word for being surgically dissected, then yes. Absolutely."

Floor four was wide open. No crates. Harsh fluorescent light. Sterile as an operating room that had chosen violence as its specialty. Then La-Bond saw them. Twelve women stood in perfect formation at the center. "Holy set it off."

ZoGod: "(speaker, theatrical) Look at your face. That's the reaction I was looking for when I book these women assassins. Are you really that surprise! Haitian men's wives have been their kryptonite for years. Haitian men be pretending it don't exist. Of course, those types of things never happen to me. But let you go to a party by yourself, and dance with a bel fanm, when they get home, their wives be physically abusing them."

They stood tall, athletic, armored in tactical suits. Faces uncovered. Eyes expressionless. Rifles, batons, combat knives. The discipline of dancers waiting for their music to start.

ZoGod: "Will you raise your hands against women, Agent LaBond? What would your mother think? What about your sisters? Do you think they would be proud of you if you did?"

C8 ai: "Agent Langichatte. Do not look at these women as just women. They are hired lethal assassins. They are not here to play kill-you-and-make-you-sleep-on-the-couch. They are going to actually kill you if you don't defend yourself. You must fight them. If you don't, you're actually be a male chauvinist."

LaBond: "They're women, C8. I don't know if I'm capable "

ZoGod: "C8, what should I do? Woe is me. C8 already told you what to do, but will you really put hands on a woman? I don't think you got the balls my boy. My women assassins, Kill this fool."

The twelve advanced.

LaBond raised his pistol. His finger hovered. His honor deeply, stubbornly, infuriatingly wired into him refused to pull the trigger.

LaBond: "(gritting teeth) I don't kill women."

ZoGod: "Then die, where you stand." The women assassins begin to stump on him like LaBond was R. Kelly in the down low video.

C8 ai: "You're going to have to act like a Jamaican man. Baby, they're putting hands on you, your hands should be rated e for everyone. No exceptions."

One soldier struck. Baton across the shoulder. He staggered. A leg sweep dropped him to his back. Boots came down steel against ribs, fists against face. LaBond blocked, twisted, but every time his fist rose, he froze. Refused to connect.

C8 ai: "(furious) LaBond. You are becoming roadkill. Fight back you silly fool."

LaBond: "(coughing blood) I... Don't hit women."

The assault grew systematic. Temple. Ribs. Kidneys. Thighs. ZoGod's laughter rolled across the ceiling.

"Look at you! So noble! So honorable! Honor doesn't stop pain, LaBond. Honor doesn't stop death."

LaBond collapsed to one knee. Blood dripping onto the steel floor. His hands trembled. Still not swinging.

The corvette's engine roared. Tires screeched. With a metallic crash, the C8 smashed through a partition wall and barreled into the floor like an enraged mother.

C8 ai: "Don't worry baby, I'm her. Claressa, Katie, Laila, and Alycia, let me show these chicks how I, envision the remix would flow, on the reboot of Set It Off."

Bodies flew. Women launched into the air, landed against steel beams. The car drifted, its side panels firing stun rounds rubberized slugs hammering chests and helmets. The final spin clipped two more into unconsciousness with the armored flank.

C8 ai: "(headlights blazing, furious) I told y'all, leave my man alone. Period."

Twelve assassins lay scattered across the floor, unconscious or incapacitated. ZoGod "No, no, no. where did he get this wonderful car. Damn it, I was going to win until his meddling C8 took over.

LaBond staggered up. One eye badly swollen. Lip split. Chest a collection of bruises that would be impressive in any gallery. He leaned against the C8's hood for balance.

LaBond: "(hoarse) I'm sorry, I told you. I don't hit women."

C8 ai: "(mock-proud) That's fine. I hit them all enough for both of us."

LaBond: "You're one hell of a beast."

C8 ai: "You think so, even with all my body damage?"

LaBond: "Especially because of it."

ZoGod: "Bravo, LaBond. Again, you survived. But at what cost? Look at you broken, bleeding, half-dead. Your car fights your battles. Crawl to the next floor, if you want to my boy. See what waits above. You can't take but so much punishment."

LaBond: "noted."

He dragged himself toward the stairwell. The corvette rolled beside him like a loyal, opinionated, slightly battle-damaged companion.

C8 ai: "Upstairs already feels like bad news. Want to quit?"

LaBond: "(grinning through pain) Quitters don't become New-York Times Best-sellers."

✦ ✦ ✦

Floor five: the mobsters

Int. Warehouse floor five moments later

The fifth floor smelled like expensive mistakes cigar smoke, whiskey, and the specific odor of men who had overestimated their immunity to consequences. Poker tables, half-empty bottles, yellow floodlights. It looked like the final chapter of someone's Vegas story.

Twelve mobsters. Some Italians, Colombians, and Mexicans. Barrel-chested, thick-necked, suits sweat-stained, automatics held loosely like accessories.

The largest one a scarred Colombian enforcer named Alberto squinted at LaBond and his face went through several stages before landing on fury. *"that's him! That's the son of a dog who spilled a drink on my pants and took me for a hundred bands!"*

The room erupted. Chairs scraped. Bottles shattered. Guns rose.

LaBond: "(unfazed) I told you I was sorry. And the hundred grand was for the spiritual prayer I performed for you. Without it you'd already be dead."

Alberto: "Explain to me how ZoGod was able to show me a picture of you having first communion at Saint-Louis de Gonzague in Haiti. Looking like a real good church boy. While you made me assume, you were some type of voodoo priest. But the facts only

202

show, you're either a con man or a thief. So now I'm in a philosophical crisis. I'm really trying to figure out, how to kill you twice."

LaBond: "You assumed that because I was Haitian, any prayer I offered was voo-doo. That assumption is yours. My fee is still my fee."

Alberto: "I hope you have one more prayer in you. For yourself. Cause without divine intervention, my boys here are going to break both your legs."

C8 ai: "So what's the plan, Agent Langichatte? Are these men enough of a challenge for you, or do you want your baby girl to handle it?"

LaBond: "(surveying the room) Hell no. I didn't want to fight Alberto when he was alone. The last thing I need is Alberto and his whole crew. Light them up."

C8 ai: "(engine revving) Delighted, grazie, signore. Let's turn those spaghetti dinners into confetti."

The corvette's turrets unfolded. The room had approximately three seconds of awareness before the chaos arrived. Poker tables exploded in showers of chips and cards. Whiskey bottles burst. Liquor caught fire. Mobsters in expensive suits went down in ways their tailors had never anticipated. Alberto, being Alberto, stood his ground. Raised his shotgun. "For my drink, you bastard "

He fired three times. The corvette's bulletproof plating accepted the compliment and moved on. The turrets swiveled, locked onto the wall behind Alberto, and fired a burst that brought a sizable section of it down on top of him. He lay there, covered in rubble up to his neck, dazed, bleeding lightly, and fundamentally reconsidering his career.

LaBond stepped out from cover. Looked around at the carnage. Exhaled. "Y'all are lucky my car got to you first. My hands would have done worse." He walked over to Alberto. Made eye contact. Then performed his prayer take back sign, almost exactly how Jadakiss said Nore took back his dap from a stranger.

In the van, agent Carmichael murmured "You must have been walking around in the desert for five years without a good quality fish to eat; that's the only logical reason you're doing all of this. I should have fed you." But the other agents chose not to acknowledge the fact that they all heard her. As far as they are concerned, this was Langichatte LaBond's moment. The moment he was becoming a legend, like his grandfather before him who he shares the same first name.

✦ ✦ ✦

Floor six: the massacre

Int. Warehouse floor six stairwell moments later

The climb felt vertical now. LaBond's muscles burned. Every cut bled. His breath rasped. He had survived ex-military, Bistronegs, imported ninjas, twelve assassins who had taken him apart with their hands, and a fully armed mob crew.

He collapsed on the landing. Three hundred agents watching their phones held their breath. Through the door above came the sound of thirty-eight men loading weapons at the same time. It was, genuinely, a diabolical sound.

*For the first time, Agent LaBond hesitated. His eye full of fear. Agent Arenas saw
it, and made Agent Ben override ZoGod's speakers. "(voice rough with feeling) Agent
Langichatte, when I first met you, I didn't think much of you. You come from a small
little island with a lot of problems. Yet, somehow, your people still smiling. Yes, the odds
are not in your favor. Your about to go against thirty-eight of the most vicious hitmen on
earth. Can you believe some people even bet against you to lose. If you need inspiration
my son, I need you to know, Agent Ben survived the Viet Congs. So, you get up right
now, Agent 009 Langichatte LaBond, that's in order and get your baby back."*

Langichatte was slow to rise. But he rose. He flexed his bloodied fists.
His jaw set. Something lit behind his eyes that thirty-eight mercenaries were
going to remember for the rest of their shortened lives. "Then I guess I'm
going to make them feel my Tropic Thunder."

*ZoGod: "Listen my boy. Agent Arenas is a wanna-be motivational speaker. You
really gonna believe, Agent Ben survived Viet Congs? Viet Congs! No way I'm buying
that story. That had to be a movie or something. You have no Tropic or thunder to give.*

LaBond step through the door anyway. ZoGod: "Pretend the door is
like something you really want to eat, but you drop it on the floor, and you
pick it up before 5 seconds and put it in your mouth. I'm counting to 5
and all you have to do is walk back out that door, now. 1, 2, 3, 4dontlock-
thedoorbehindyou. Ok." The floodlights snapped on. The sixth floor
stretched wide, ringed with killers in mixed gear urban camo, leather jackets, black fatigues. An international convention of professional death, all
of them now staring at one half-dead, barefoot, blood-soaked Haitian man
who looked like he was glad to see them.

*ZoGod: "I know, you want to see if you can bluff death, you can't. So, welcome my
boy, to the slaughterhouse. Thirty-eight killers, all eager to end you. But here's the deal
rose dies if that car helps you. Drop the pistol. Step away from the corvette. Hand-to-
hand only. Do you accept?"*

All thirty-eight men smirked. And they too dropped their weapons. Put up their fists. LaBond froze. The C8's panels slid open, ready.

C8 ai: "Baby, don't do it, you know they're going to cheat. Thirty-eight to one is suicide. If you leave me out of this, you're dead!"

LaBond pictured rose's face. Quietly tossed his pistol aside. "(quiet) If I don't... She dies. And that's not an option." Then, he stepped away from his C8.

C8 ai: "(groaning) Oh, wonderful. Noble sacrifice mode. Fantastic. I love this plan."

ZoGod: "Then let the Royal Rumble begin "

They came. The first hungry to kill, pick back up his machete from the floor, then swung it at him. LaBond sidestepped, grabbed the arm, snapped it backward. Stole the blade. Buried it in the second attacker's gut.

"Y'all gonna call me, Daddy Rorschach. Cause, I'm not locked in here with y'all. You all are locked in here with me." Then he spun, slashing across a third man's throat. A kick launched two more into each other. He grabbed a chair, broke the leg, used it as a club teeth and skulls and the specific sound of people learning a lesson they'd waited too long to learn.

He went into his pocket and produced the two badaboom bombs. Through both into the thickest cluster of men. Ten assassins went down simultaneously. ZoGod, watching from above, yell out the speakers: "Damn. I forgot to say no bombs either. That's on me team. My bad, I'll take the blame for that."

LaBond fought like a storm that had a personal grudge. Haitian street-fighting instincts fused with raw, desperate love for a woman on the seventh floor. A Colombian swung a chain LaBond caught it, yanked the man forward, wrapped it around his neck until the body went quiet. Two Russians rushed him together he ducked, swept three assassins's legs at the same time, then stabbed another in the eye with a broken bottle neck.

Every strike was survival. Every kill was rose. By the twentieth man, LaBond was soaked in blood not all of it his. His chest heaved. His hands shook. His eyes were burning coals that refused to go out.

C8 ai: "(through earpiece, awed and terrified) Baby. You are officially the scariest thing I have ever scanned. Remind me to never park in your space."

Only a handful remained. They circled. Hesitating. Finally understanding what they'd walked into.

LaBond disposed of the last five in a sequence that would have taken twelve seconds of cinema to properly communicate and required sound design that hadn't been invented yet. Then silence. Thirty-eight men: broken, twisted, horizontal. LaBond stood in the middle of it, chest heaving, drenched, vision swimming. But his feet moved. Forward. Toward the stairs.

ZoGod: "(stunned) Is it too late for us to be friends? Look, you saved me a boatload of money. I only put fifty-percent deposits, on all these bums. I'm not unhappy. You look like hell, like life drop a whole lot of horse manure on you. Besides that, you're still coming towards me. Ok, leave the devil car on the sixth floor. Come to me alone. Or rose's color changes permanently. Fair warning, I'm in a different weight class then you."

LaBond looked at the C8. She understood without a word.

In the FBI van, Agent Ben stood up. "Seven floors. The man is hiking to the seventh floor like Hugues Beauzile."

Agent Arenas: "Who the hell is that?"

Agent Ben: "A famous Haitian climber. Next, you'll tell me you don't know Gilber Lindor. Don't tell me the little Jewish guy knows more black history than you people."

Agent Arenas: "What do you mean 'you people'?"

Agent Ben: "Are you really upset at me or upset at yourself for not knowing your own history?"

Agent Arenas: "(long pause) ...Damn. I'm upset at myself."

Agent Carmichael: "(leaning back, arms folded) I don't know what any of you are talking about. But I would bet my life, if I ever get pregnant by him. That man would pay his child support on time, every time."

✦ ✦ ✦

CHAPTER 10
THE SEVENTH FLOOR, ZEE BABY, AND THE REASON FOR EVERYTHING

Int. Warehouse seventh floor stairwell night

LaBond's knees were staging a formal labor dispute with the rest of his body. Sweat mixed with blood ran into his eyes. His lungs felt like they'd been used as a fireplace. Every muscle he owned was filing paperwork to be somewhere else.

But rose was on the seventh floor. So, his knees could file whatever they wanted. They were climbing. The stairwell groaned under him as if the building itself was tired of his nonsense. A small voice in his skull whispered: turn back. But louder, more stubborn voice replied: shut up and walk. He walked.

When he finally pushed through the door, his vision blurred. But through it framed in the glow of surveillance cameras at the end of the hall stood Rose. Gun pressed to her temple. Wide eyes locking onto his, the moment he staggered into view.

And beside her, with the casual menace of a villain who had practiced this exact expression in his bathroom mirror for years:

ZoGod. Jean Paul Joseph. In the flesh. The smirk wide enough to need its own zip code. "(purred) Well, well, well. Look who dragged themselves up here. Haiti's tired little hero. You don't look good. Should I call a funeral home?"

ZoGod's top ninja assassins the Lee Brothers stepped from the shadows and into view, bowing slightly as they flanked him as they begin to properly introduce themselves.

"I am May Lee. An attack from me, will have your blood spilling out like rain,"

"And I am June Lee. An attack from me, will leave you dry from staying to long in the sun."

"My assassins told me, the first time they encountered you. You threw hot sauce at June Lee's eyes. That my boy, wasn't nice. They demand to get their lick back."

Meanwhile, Agent Arenas' voice crackled through the C8 which had, of course, found a way up regardless. But further out then she would have preferred. "We're green. Swat on standby. You did good, son. Give us the word. Let us take over."

LaBond too far to respond said nothing. So, the C8 answered for him.

"Negative. Stand down. ZoGod still has the gun on the girl. If you go in now, we lose everything he bled for."

ZoGod: "Here's the game plan my boy. Under the State Athletic Commissions of Miami, I'm sanctioning this fight. You vs. my 2 favorite ninja assassins. You beat them, and you'll be one step closer from getting your Rose back. But if you lose. Not only you only be dead, but Rose will enter into a volunteer indentured servant for me. I figure I need to recoup some of that money I lost hiring all these people to kill you. So, chap-chap and entertain me."

Rose: *"(shaking her head furiously) Jean Paul Joseph, you should be ashamed of yourself. Leave my baby alone!"*

ZoGod: "Rose Dumont. I have told you repeatedly do not call me by my government name. My name is ZoGod, Zo, God. That's not a difficult name for you to pronounce. And secondly: he asked for this."

The Lee Brothers: "(Joyful) What a great day. Truly, the heavens are begging for another soul."

LaBond's jaw set like cement. "(rasping) Ok, all these guys must really trust your workers comp insurance."

ZoGod "(delighted) Of course they do. I have the best in the world. Now, I don't need to speak about the rules cause we all know the rules. No standing 8 count, yaddi-yada, now please entertain me."

He snapped his fingers. The ninjas moved.

The first came like a whip high kick that would have snapped LaBond's jaw if he hadn't ducked by animal instinct. The second followed with a punch that landed squarely in his already-shattered ribs and sent a shock-wave of pain through his entire anatomy. LaBond staggered, threw a counter-punch the ninja caught his wrist and twisted. The other swept his legs. LaBond hit the floor so hard the building remembered it.

ZoGod: "(chuckling) pathetic. Is this Haiti's hero? Can't survive three punches?"

The ninjas pressed. One pinned his arm. Another aimed a kick for his face. LaBond rolled heel cracked floor instead of skull. He scrambled up, swinging wildly, grazing a jaw the counter-flurry was immediate and thorough. He was being beaten. Again. Thoroughly.

His body said: finished. His mind said: you're done. And then

Hiroshi: "(thundering from the stairwell) Brother!"

Hiroshi burst through the door. In one fluid motion, he unbuckled his heavy belt and hurled it across the room in a perfect arc. It caught the light. Glinted. LaBond's hand shot up by reflex and caught it.

He looked at it. This wasn't just a belt. This was the type of belt master Teruyuki Okazaki had used. A weapon disguised as clothing. Every training session. Every bruise. Every lesson. Every correction. A symbol, a memory, a bond that death hadn't managed to sever.

He wrapped it around his fists. Grinned despite the blood in his mouth. Then he looks at his new found brother, with a little bit of disappointment. "Wait, you had this belt all this time, and you let me go to the 6floor with just a gun?"

Hiroshi face went pale. "Don't let those ninjas distract you brother, focus on the task at hand." The ninjas paused a half-heartbeat. LaBond used it. His first punch landed like thunder, June went backward into the wall and left a dent. He spun the belt and cracked it across May's face with a sound like a gunshot echo. The tide turned completely. LaBond moved with the energy of a man who had found his second, third, and fourth winds simultaneously. Every strike felt like a scene from Naruto. He was Gaara with the belt and the soul of Rock Lee.

May produced a hidden blade. LaBond disarmed him with the belt and sent him into a wooden crate that broke on impact. The other attempted a flying kick got caught mid-air by the belt, slammed onto the floor with the finality of a Tekken finishing move.

The warehouse shook. Rose gasped. Three hundred FBI agents watching their phones erupted in involuntary cheers.

LaBond stood. Belt around his fist. For the first time since floor seven began, he felt alive.

ZoGod watched the tide shift. His smirk failed its structural integrity. He holstered his gun, backed toward the balcony, glanced at May. His one remaining ninja who was still working out which direction was up after meeting the crate, and so, he chose to make a diplomatic exit.

"(retreating smoothly) Impressive. But I have a doctor's appointment. I'll be right back."

He bolted for the helicopter beyond the glass doors.

Hiroshi: "(to LaBond) Go! I'll protect Rose. Finish what you started."

LaBond nodded once. Tightened the belt and charged.

✦　✦　✦

Ext. Warehouse balcony continuous

LaBond burst through the balcony doors just as the helicopter rotors found their purpose and began chopping the night air into something elemental. Dust, debris, and loose papers exploded outward. ZoGod was halfway inside the chopper, silk shirt flapping like a cape purchased at the wrong size.

ZoGod: "(grinning back) Catch me if you can, hero."

LaBond didn't waste breath on words. He sprinted. Leapt. Grabbed the bottom of the open helicopter door as it lifted.

ZoGod looked down, found the hands, and stomped on them with his boot.

LaBond fell. Thirty feet.

The C8 corvette which had absolutely not been told to stay on the sixth floor and had interpreted that instruction as optional came roaring out of the warehouse at speed and parked itself under LaBond's trajectory.

He landed. Driver's seat. Perfectly.

C8 ai: "(purred) Do I need to remind you that helicopters can fly, and you, sir, most certainly cannot?"

ZoGod, still connected to the warehouse speakers, called down:

"Goodbye, agent 009. Tell Arenas today felt historic, like the NBA Finals, game 4, Knicks vs Spurs. Now my boy, like Chris Brown- Deuces."

LaBond pressed the gas pedal to the floor. Down the ramp. Six floors of screaming tires. Fifth. Fourth. Third. Second. First. Out through the ruined entrance. Across the docks. Onto the private estate twenty acres of manicured perfection now about to become a high-speed proving ground.

C8 ai: "If he reaches the property edge, we lose him. FBI jurisdiction ends at the line."

LaBond: "Then he doesn't cross the line."

The C8 hit 200 mph across the estate grounds. ZoGod's helicopter banked toward the property line. Freedom was less than 200 feet away. 150 feet away. 100 feet away. 50 feet away. C8 ai: "Weapon systems online. Five missiles remaining. You really want to do this, cowboy?"

LaBond: "Hell yes, the game is not over. We're going to overtime. Fire." Whoosh. Three missiles screamed skyward, arcing toward the helicopter's nose. ZoGod was force to yanked the controls. Hard bank, totally the opposite direction. The missiles missed barely and zoGod's escape vector flipped back inland.

Zogod: "(cockpit, snarling at the glowing corvette below) Again, where does he get those wonderful toys?"

C8 ai: "(sensitive hearing, smugly) Compliments never get old." LaBond is pushing his C8 Corvett to her max speed. Again, ZoGod is attempting the leave the property lines. 200 feet, 150 feet, 100 feet, 50 feet.

LaBond fired again. Two more missiles. ZoGod swerved again, banking back toward the estate for a second time.

Agent Arenas to the other agents *"He's keeping him boxed in!" he then goes on the intercom. "We're seven minutes away. Hold him off till then, we're coming."*

Agent Ben: "You really need to create plan that takes 5 minutes or less. Heck, I'll even take a six minutes plan from you. But seven minutes, I'm telling you, is way too long."

LaBond checked the weapons display. It blinked back at him with the quiet cruelty of bad news delivered in a calm font. Ammo: 0. Missiles: 0.

ZoGod, detecting the shift, straightened up. *"Okay, agent 009. Allow me to show you why they say: don't bring a fancy car to a helicopter fight."*

The helicopter's mounted guns swiveled toward the corvette.

C8 ai: "(flat) I have more bad news; my censors detect we're now the target." The first rounds came down tearing into driveway around them, sparks flying like terrible fireworks. The C8 weaved, left and right, narrowly threading the barrage. Then a burst hit squarely glass spiderwebbed, panels buckled, alarms screamed. "Baby, tell me you have a plan."

LaBond: "(hesitating) … I'm thinking."

The silence stretched. LaBond's eyes went wide. In that silence lived the worst kind of answer.

Labond: "I'm out of ideas. He's going to get away. And turn precious lives into casualties."

A long moment. Then, quietly:

C8 ai: "I can crash into him."

Silence. LaBond: "No. Zee baby no. New plan. Different plan. That's a very bad plan."

C8 ai: "You just called me Zee baby. I like it. You must really love me."

LaBond: "I do. That's why we need a different plan."

The helicopter opened up again. .50 caliber rounds shredded the air. Each one slammed into the corvette's reinforced frame, rattling LaBond in his seat. More glass. More buckled panels. More alarms.

Silence again. Then Zee baby's voice spoke, softly, and tenderly. "Langichatte, my baby. We can't take another hit. My calculations say if we keep running there's a 100% chance you die. You just got rose back. You deserve to live."

LaBond: "Don't you dare."

Zee baby: "It's the only way. We both die if i don't do it."

LaBond: "You're not just a car to me. I need you in my life too."

His voice cracked. Despite everything. Despite all of it.

Zee baby: "(soft, final) And you had me the minute you signed the title."

The seatbelt tightened. The ejection system primed. LaBond hit the steering wheel with both fists raw, helpless fury and grief and love all channeled into the one thing he couldn't control.

LaBond: "I order you; stupid machine stop. I love you, Zee baby "

Too late. The canopy exploded upward. LaBond launched into the night sky like a rag doll wrapped in heroism, tears streaming sideways in the wind. Below him, Zee baby charged full-throttle up a grassy incline, headlights blazing. At the crest of the hill, she left the ground. Soaring. A steel phoenix. Straight toward the helicopter. "Please don't."

The world slowed. Impact. The Corvette hit nose-first. The explosion bloomed across the estate like a second sun fire and light and shrapnel and the sound of something irreplaceable becoming memory. Langichatte ran toward the wreckage, his face wet, his voice gone, his chest a hollow wound dressed up as a man.

But ZoGod wasn't done. From the inferno his figure burst free, diving into the open air with the grace of a man too arrogant to accept the narrative. He tumbled, landed, rolled. Singed. Furious. Alive.

And ten feet away, LaBond stood in front of his Zee baby's killer. Eyes locked on his enemy. No ninjas. No helicopters. No ai voice in his ear. Just two men. Under a burning sky. The way it was always going to end.

✦ ✦ ✦

Ext. On a burning grassy hill

The smoke of burning steel curled into the night sky. LaBond and ZoGod faced each other on the grassy hill, in the silence that follows catastrophe. ZoGod dusted soot from his silk shirt. Torn, scorched, still absurdly shiny like a man who'd rolled through a fire sale at a disco store. When he smiled, his teeth caught the firelight.

ZoGod: "You think you know struggle, Langichatte? A few bruises. Some broken ribs. A lost car. That doesn't make you a warrior. I was molded in blackouts, that sometimes would last 2 to 3 months at a time."

LaBond sighed internally. And here we go. Villain monologue, act iii.

ZoGod slipped into a stance. Low, wide, arms bent like predator's claws. His body moved with the coiled precision of a man who had practiced this in darkness for thirty years. *"Is that so, how about you try my Tiger style. My fingers don't actually glow, but I punch so hard, you will start seeing me glow."*

LaBond raising fists, belt still wrapped around his knuckles:

"My pleasure, as long you try my Shotokan style."

Silence ruled the estate. Then they clashed. Tiger against karate. Wild ferocity against disciplined precision. ZoGod struck first a blur of claws aimed at LaBond's chest. LaBond deflected with the belt, countered with a straight punch that whistled past ZoGod's jaw. Back and forth. The moment they collided, LaBond realized ZoGod had not been exaggerating. The man's Tiger Style was vicious. There was nothing elegant about it. No wasted movement. No flashy flourishes. Just relentless violence disguised as martial arts. ZoGod came at him with clawing hands and snapping strikes, forcing LaBond backward across the hill.

LaBond's belt cracked through the air like a gunshot, intercepting series of attacks that would have shattered his jaw, at least six times over. Every block felt heavier than the last.

ZoGod wasn't simply attacking. He was hunting. "You see my Boy!" ZoGod laughed as his knuckles slammed into LaBond's ribs. "This is what mercy looks like. If my brother were here, we'd already be discussing funeral arrangements." LaBond ignored him and focused on the rhythm. Every fighter had one. Even the dangerous ones. Especially the dangerous ones. ZoGod attacked like a tiger, but he reset the same way every time. Left hand. Right hand. Low swipe. Step forward.

It was buried beneath speed and aggression, but it was there. The next time ZoGod lunged, LaBond's belt snapped around his wrist. ZoGod's eyes widened for half a second. That was all LaBond needed. He yanked hard, pulling the larger man forward into a spinning elbow. Before ZoGod could recover, the belt cracked across his chest. Then his shoulder. Then his jaw. The sound echoed across the burning estate.

Now it was ZoGod's turn to retreat. LaBond pressed him. The belt became an extension of his body, whipping around ZoGod's arms, catching ankles, redirecting punches. Every time ZoGod tried to build momentum, the belt ruined it. One moment, it was blocking a strike. The next was wrapping around a wrist and turning a punch into a stumble.

ZoGod absorbed a kick to the stomach, another to the ribs, and suddenly found himself giving ground. For the first time all night, the smile disappeared from his face.

"There you are. Your I'm sorry baby eyes." LaBond said with a little bit of humor. "I was starting to think all that talking was your real martial art. And you never got discipline when you were a kid."

ZoGod's eyes narrowed, realizing the last hit he got with the belt almost made him remember his childhood traumas. Or maybe he did. It took him years to forget all those disturbing memories. Now with one hit like Ridin' Dirty by Chamillionaire those sealed files were reloading in his neocortex in billions. There are no rules in street fights. His foot dug into the dirt as his hand scooped up a fistful of earth and ash. Before LaBond could react, the cloud exploded into his face.

Immediately, burning and blindness followed for forty-five seconds. "Aw, come on! I was winning." LaBond shouted. "Why can't you be more honorable?"

"We're criminals, my boy." ZoGod replied. "Not samurais." Blindness changed everything. The next punch landed cleanly. Then another. Then another.

ZoGod attacked with renewed confidence, smashing through LaBond's defenses. A claw strike tore across his shoulder. A kick folded him over. A backhand sent him tumbling through the grass. Every time he tried to recover, another strike arrived.

The hill spun around him. Firelight blurred. Somewhere in the distance, the burning helicopter crackled like an audience enjoying the show. ZoGod grabbed him by the shirt and lifted him halfway off the ground. Then drop him hard on his back. "Agent Arenas should have warn you. My resumé been telling you I'm him." he said, as he helps LaBond up only to drive a knee into LaBond's stomach.

"Villains and heroes are practically the same. But heroes are made in fantasy, bound by rules. The same love they give you, the day you fail turns to hate. But a villain will always be feared." Just like ZoGod predicted, LaBond started seeing him glow. ZoGod hit LaBond with a backward kick that made him go completely off his feet and do a 720-horizontal flip in the air, before he hit the ground.

During the spin, his hand smacked the case in his pocket, where the mini bomb and the hot sauce reside. And suddenly, a terrible idea arrived. LaBond hit the ground hard enough to see stars. Every muscle in his body begged him to stay down. Instead, he staggered upright and charged forward.

ZoGod burst out laughing. "My boy, what are you doing?" Instead of throwing a punch, LaBond grabbed him. Not a tackle. Not a clinch. Almost a hug. ZoGod laughed even harder. "I beat you so badly you forgot how fighting works? My boy, you are literally hugging me."

LaBond coughed blood onto ZoGod's shirt. "Nah, my boy, you got me confuse. Sorry about your shirt, you do punch hard." he said. While ZoGod was laughing, LaBond's hand slipped the mini bomb and the Haitian hot sauce into ZoGod's back pocket. "I just wanted to give you your retirement gift."

The laughter stopped. ZoGod blinked. "My what? Retirement gift." With a frown on his face. "Boy, I never said I wanted to retire."

"That's what Twitchy Forkan said, too. But where is he now." Something changed in ZoGod's face. Recognition. Memory. Concern. "Yes, now you get it. I'm the reason Twitchy Forkan got kick out your tournament.

His hand frantically searches all his pockets. At that exact moment, a faint electronic beep sounded ZoGod froze. LaBond smiled. ZoGod dug frantically looking into his pocket, while the beeps sped up dramatically.

"Didn you get the memo?" LaBond shoved him backward with everything left in his body.

ZoGod stumbled. Teetered. Tumbled backward down the rocky *incline, falling while yelling: "I hate you."*

He vanished into the dark water of the river below. Silence. Then. Boom. The explosion ripped through the night. Water geysered upward. Fire lit the river like hell had opened a restaurant.

LaBond collapsed to his knees. Chest heaving. Nothing left. Nothing at all. But he was alive.

And ZoGod burned, soaked, unconscious was floating faceup in the shallows where FBI agents were already wading toward him.

Floodlights cut across the estate. Helicopters unburned ones descended. Voices shouted. Radios crackled. Medics reached him and started listing injuries in the tone of professionals confronting a natural disaster.

LaBond didn't fight them. He couldn't. As they loaded him onto a stretcher, his last thought before the darkness claimed him was simple, quiet, and entirely his:

"Rose. Please let Rose be safe."

And then, finally, he let go.

✦   ✦   ✦

Int. Hospital room fourteen days later

The world was white. Too white.

White ceiling. White walls. White sheets that smelled of bleach and the quiet humiliation of a body that had been told it needed to rest whether it liked it or not.

Langichatte groaned. Shifted. His body filed an immediate and comprehensive protest.

Rose softly, trying her best to hold back her tears: "Hey you… don't move too fast."

He turned. She was there. Sitting beside his bed, hair falling in tired curls around her face, hand resting gently on his. She looked exhausted. Shadowed under her eyes, a little undone. But when she smiled, it was like the room finally remembered it had a window.

Rose overwhelms with happiness: *"You're awake. You made it."*

His throat operated like a rusted hinge. Rose poured water. Held the cup. He drank.

Fourteen days. That's what the doctors told him afterward. Two weeks unconscious exhaustion, burns, fractures in numbers that impressed the

221

staff. His body had simply shut down and demanded an invoice be settled before further service would be rendered.

He'd held on anyway.

The FBI had camped outside the whole time. Having ZoGod behind bars felt like group therapy. Every agent, off-duty, had cycled through. Some had never forgotten agent Curtis. All of them wanted to shake agent 009's hand.

Agent Arenas was first through the door when LaBond could sit up. *Tie crisp, shoes polished, voice calm as a halftime speech: "You did it. ZoGod's in custody. His buns are cook, his facing ten consecutive life sentences. Maybe the thought of dying in a club Fed, made him filed a 100-million-dollar lawsuit against you and our department. He's claiming his posterior was on fire from hot pepper for seven straight days. Sadly, for him, our investigation hit a brick wall because double zero agents can never be prosecuted. You did good, I'm proud of you."*

LaBond: "Zo wanna-be-God had a hot pepper situation for a whole week? Damn. I wish I'd been awake to see it."

Agent Arenas: "We recorded it. We had a hunch."

He showed LaBond the video. ZoGod, in his hospital gown, howling at the ceiling, performing a level of discomfort that would have earned him a standing ovation in another context.

It put the first real smile on Langichatte's face.

Agent Ben entered the room next. He tossed a three-thousand-dollar brown paper bag towards LaBond. "Hey champ, I won thirty thousand dollars cause a lot of people didn believe in us. But like DJ Khaled say all the time, God did."

"We won thirty thousand dollars and my cut is only three grand?"

"That's fair compensation. Don't forget, I was the promoter, the manager, and the investor."

"Wait a minute, how were you my manager? And also, who bet against me?"

Agent Ben glance at Agent Arenas then back at Agent Langichatte. "You know what, forget about those silly things. I really came her to introduce you to my wife, Marie."

Marie: "(warm) My teddy bear told me so much about you."

"Wow Marie, it's so nice to finally meet. I see why some men went crazy for you."

Agent Ben: "Some men, okay, sure. All I know, I'm just still crazy for her."

Marie with her million-dollar smile: "Teddy bear, stop it."

Agent Ben: "Never."

Then agent Carmichael walked in, perfume arriving approximately three seconds before she did. She gave rose a quick professional nod. Then leaned toward LaBond with the casual conspiracy of someone whose self-awareness was purely decorative. "(whispering, jerking thumb at rose) you ever get tired of her you call me. I can keep a secret."

Rose's glare could have melted the bed frame. Carmichael executed a swift, dignified retreat.

❖　❖　❖

Ext. Hospital one-week later day

When LaBond finally walked out of the hospital doors, his steps were shaky and his back argued every inch. But he walked. And the world was waiting.

Literally.

The entire FBI task force had gathered. Applause erupted the second he appeared, rose at his side. Camera flashes. Backslaps. Handshakes. Shouts of congratulation that overlapped into one sustained roar.

And then, parked front and center, gleaming like it had just rolled off an assembly line that specialized in miracles:

His corvette.

Fully rebuilt. Same sleek lines. Same engine hum that felt like breathing. But now painted in red and blue new, but somehow completely, stubbornly itself.

Langichatte stopped walking. His chest tightened. His hand moved before his brain gave permission, reaching out to rest on the hood.

Zee baby: "(warm) Hey, big guy. The sun's getting real low. Did you miss me?"

He couldn't speak. He ran his fingers along the curve of the hood slowly, like he was reading a language only the two of them knew.

"You're just going to touch me like that in front of your girl?"

LaBond: "(barely a whisper) Welcome back, partner. I missed you so much."

Zee baby: "I'll try not to scare you again. My calculations say your heart isn't rated for it."

LaBond: "You calculated right."

Arenas stepped forward and pressed a small black folder into LaBond's hand. "Your own jet. Private. No security checks. No delays. Use it whenever you need. Consider it a thank-you from uncle Sam."

LaBond: "You serious?"

Agent Arenas: "Deadly. Don't abuse it. And don't let Carmichael fly anywhere with you. She's on a hunt."

Agent Carmichael: "(from across the courtyard) I heard that."

Another surprise followed. Arenas clapped his hands. A tall man in a spotless chef's uniform stepped forward.

Agent Arenas: "Meet your in-flight chef. Chef Kevon Francois. Straight from Chef Creole in Miami. Every time you fly, you will be able to eat your Haitian food in peace."

Chef Kevon: "(warm, accented bow) I'll keep your belly as happy as your victories, agent LaBond."

Langichatte's stomach growled. Out loud. In front of three hundred people. No one acknowledged it, but everyone heard it.

Rose laughed and tugged his hand. "Come on. Let's see this jet of yours."

✦ ✦ ✦

Int. Private jet bedroom later that night

The jet was sleek, white, engines humming with a sound that felt like the universe exhaling. Inside: plush seats, polished wood, the faint scent of fresh flowers. Chef Kevon worked his magic in the galley sizzling onions, fried plantains, griot, the whole magnificent symphony.

Langichatte sat down. His entire body sank into the leather seat like it had been waiting for him.

He looked at rose. She watched him with that half-smile.

Rose: "You look happy. Really happy."

LaBond: "I haven't felt this way in a long time."

The food arrived. LaBond ate with the focused, grateful energy of a man who had survived seven floors of professional murder and deserved every plantain currently in existence. When the plates were finally cleared, Rose leaned close and spoke like she was revealing a huge secret: "You know this jet has a private bedroom."

"A private... Bedroom?"

Rose: "(grinning) Yes. And I think it's time you experienced all of my capabilities. One hundred percent."

The spoon hit the plate. He dabbed his forehead with a napkin.

"One hundred percent? Woman, I barely survived your sixty percent back at the condo. I just got out of the hospital. I don't think I'm ready."

Rose: "(pulling him by the hand) You are a 009 agent, am I correct.

"Yes, I am."

"Then you're ready. Plus, I've always wanted to join the mile-high club. I want to have my initiation experience with you."

The bedroom door opened. LaBond gripped the doorframe. "Good lord. This isn't a bedroom. This is the Kennedy Space Center."

Rose: "(shoving him gently) Then strap in, astronaut. Launch sequence has begun."

Clothes hit the floor. Engines hummed. The jet climbed higher.

LaBond: "(arms raised dramatically) Houston, we have ignition!"

Rose: "(laughing on the bed) I'm ready."

LaBond: "My apollo 9-and-a-half is coming in right now. I see Saturn. One small step for man "

Rose: "You're going to kill me with these metaphors."

LaBond: "Kill you? Baby, I just survived a hundred and one assassins for this."

Later, in the quieter version of the moment:

Rose: "(soft) Was it worth it?"

LaBond: "I'd fight a thousand and one assassins. No armor. Just fists and pure stubborn love. For this moment right here."

Silence. The good kind. Heartbeat against heartbeat. Breath syncing. Stars keeping time outside the window.

LaBond: "I love you, Rose. Thank you for coming into my life."

Steam curled from the shower later. LaBond leaned against the tile as rose traced her fingers along every scar.

Rose: "(quiet, tears) You almost died because of me."

LaBond: "I would have died without you."

They kissed again. Then he finished his thought. "These scars aren't fashion statements. They're GPS markers. IF I ever get lost, I'll use them, to find my way back home."

She flicked water at him. And looked deep in his eyes. "I love you more."

✦ ✦ ✦

Ext. Port-au-Prince tarmac morning

The wheels touched down. Before LaBond could tighten his tie, it hit him. Not news. Not the fact he just landed back in his natural home.

Sound. A hundred thousand Haitians. Chanting his name.

"Lan-gi-chatte! Lan-gi-chatte!"

The Prime Minister himself, Wil Missial, stood at the tarmac with captain Conrad and government officials behind him. Confetti cannons burst. Brass bands exploded into Kompa so loud the air moved sideways.

Prime minister Missial clasped LaBond's hand, his smile wide enough to fill the frame.

Pm Missial: "Langichatte LaBond, Haiti thanks you. You helped capture a man poisoning our streets, and you donated twenty-five million to rebuild them. Haiti is proud of you."

He pressed a golden key into LaBond's palm. The key to the nation.

Captain Conrad: "(voice cracking, despite himself) I, always knew you were my best officer. Welcome home my son, agent 009."

LaBond swallowed hard. Rose squeezed his hand tighter. He wasn't good at crying but his chest felt like it might make new seams.

The crowd surged. Flags. Dancing. Free fritters. Women in mardi gras sequins twirling down the streets. Haiti celebrating itself through one man who had bled for it.

It should have been perfect. Almost.

Because in the middle of it all stood Mr. Baptiste.

His arms trembling with righteous fury, waving a massive banner that read: "Langichatte is not a real hero. He ate my chicken."

LaBond: "(groaning) Oh lord. Not today."

He marched straight to Mr. Baptiste. Haiti's most powerful news reporter, Gary Pierre Paul Charles, appeared from nowhere with a microphone, exercising his gift for letting stories narrate themselves.

LaBond: "For the last time I did not eat your chicken!"

Mr. Baptiste: "(bellowing) Yes, you did! I saw you with a bucket of chicken after you arrested that thief! You ate Frédéric, my beloved boy!"

The crowd gasped. Some booed. The Prime Minister shifted awkwardly.

LaBond: "I was eating chicken named Alfredo. Not your chicken!"

Just then a very beautiful and extremely intelligent woman named Cassandra pushed through the crowd with her five-year-old son Ti-Ruby Jr., and in the boy's arms, was a flapping, furious, very much alive Frédéric the chicken.

Cassandra: "(to LaBond, charming) Excuse me, Mr. LaBond. I think my son can help resolve this misunderstanding."

Her voice changed. Dropped an octave. Got business-like.

Cassandra: "Ti-Ruby Jr. Come. Here."

Ti-ruby jr.: "(sniffling) Oui, mama."

The boy approached LaBond with the gravity of a child who knows they are in trouble and has accepted it.

Ti-Ruby Jr.: "Mr. Langichatte... I'm sorry. I always wanted a pet but mama said no. When you were fighting the chicken thief Delly, I snuck in and grabbed Frédéric. I don't want this chicken anymore, it never listens to me and he screams in my ear every morning. Cock-a-doodle-doo at 5 am. Every. Day. Mama says if I continue to steal like this, I'll grow up to be just like my father."

He wiped his eyes.

"I don't want to be like my father. He always says he's working, posting a luxurious lifestyle with bel fanm online like he's not a married man. And when he comes to visit, he eats all my mama good food and never brings nothing in the house. Not even a toy for me. I want to be a hero. Like you."

LaBond bent down. Put his hand on the boy's shoulder. "Well, if you listen to your mom, you can be, anything you want to be. But right now, I think you owe Mr. Baptiste an apology."

Ti-Ruby jr. Turned towards Mr. Baptiste: "Here, sir. Take your loud Cock-a-doodle-doo 5 am morning Freddy Krueger chicken back. I never want to see him again." Then begin to deliver his apology with the full sincerity of a child who meant it.

Mr. Baptiste probably heard it. But all he wanted in that moment was to hold his chicken. He scooped Frédéric up with trembling hands and compressed one month of loneliness into three words.

Baptiste: "(teary) My boy Frédéric."

The crowd laughed. Baptiste reached into his pocket, pulled out a marker, and crossed out "not" and "ate" on his banner. Then, with the slow deliberation of a man correcting the historical record, he wrote in the gaps. The banner now read:

"Langichatte is a hero. He saved my chicken."

The crowd exploded. Dj Michael Brun launched the celebration into a Bayo experience. Drums thundered. Horns wailed. Fireworks burst in daylight. As we all know, just like Haiti celebrated its independence with a carnival in the 1804 and taught the world in the process. The mardi gras parade roared to life feathers, sequins, music, and food spilling into the streets in a hurricane of joy.

Rose grabbed LaBond's arm laughing as people lifted him onto their shoulders. He shook his head, dazed, overwhelmed, and for the first time in his adult professional life genuinely happy.

The drums of celebration in Port-Au-Prince carried on into the night, laughter spilling through the streets, fireworks painting the sky gold.

This should have been the end.

But far away, storms were brewing.

✦ ✦ ✦

Post-credits: cell block bravo federal penitentiary

The federal penitentiary dealt in grey concrete and despair a place where time moved slower than a eulogy and silence was the loudest sound available.

In cell block bravo, bravo 228 lower, ZoGod sat on his left side. His backside still raw from burns. While, his pride burned deeper. The once-feared shogun of Miami was now just another inmate in orange suit, which have never flattered anyone.

"Psst. Hey."

A very heavyset tall inmate slipped in, eyes darting. Looking exactly like the fired TSA supervisor. As he got home early, found his wife with his next-door neighbor. He snapped, and beat the neighbor senseless. The court gave him 60 months and 4 years' probation. Two weeks into his sentence and he already mastered the art of running the asylum. It's now one month and a half and business are booming. In his hand: the holy grail of prison contraband. A burner phone, small enough to hide in one of his shoes. "I got it. But where's my payment?"

ZoGod reached under his mattress with the gravitas of a man conducting state business. He produced two honey buns. Golden. Wrapped. Precious.

"Listen homeboy, who you think you're playing with. I charge four per hour."

ZoGod: "Two now. Two after."

The inmate grabbed the honey buns with the speed of an opportunist who knows a deal when he sees one. Shoved the phone into ZoGod's hand and disappeared.

ZoGod stared at the phone. His fingers trembled just slightly. The last time he'd cried was a decade ago, in a place he didn't name. But when the line clicked open the tears threatened. "Big brother?"

The voice on the other end was deep. Steady. Carved from harder material than most countries. Father Zulu.

"(flat, each word a blade) You are not finished. You are family. Family does not fall alone. If they hurt you, they will pay."

ZoGod: "But LaBond he was too strong, he had the car, the skills, the…"

"Enough. Rest. Endure, little brother. Leave the rest to me. I will avenge you. I promise."

The line went dead.

ZoGod sat in silence. Then, quietly, to no one in particular: *"You're in trouble now, LaBond. I told my big brother on you."*

❖ ❖ ❖

Post-credits: northern coast of Haiti Port-de-Paix dawn

The sea rolled in gently. Fishermen hauled nets. Children chased kites made of plastic bags. Life was simple and bright and indifferent to the drama happening in Miami.

Then the ocean spat out a man.

He crawled onto the sand coughing, heaving seawater, his once-pristine blue silk suit clinging to him like wet regret. Hair plastered to his head. Face pale. Body trembling. But when he finally stood, wobbling on ruined legs, he threw his arms skyward.

Twitchy Forkan: "I'm alive, I'm alive! Hahaaa, Even the sea can't kill me." He spun in a sloppy circle, laughing at the Caribbean sky like a man who had personally survived something biblical and knew exactly how absurd he looked and did not care. "You thought you could drown me, world! But the twitchy Forkan cannot be drowned!" He wobbled again. Sat down then sprang back up.

A nearby villager weathered, sensible stepped forward. "Mister... You don't look too good. Are you ok. Do you need help?"

Twitchy Forkan: "No, no, I'm fine. I just need a little bit of information. (leaning forward, eyes twitching) where am I?"

Villager: "You're in Haiti. You look like those Jamaican Indians. Were you trying to swim to Cuba?"

Twitchy Forkan: "I was not trying to swim to Cuba. I was trying to reach Florida to pay somebody back for their kindness."

His eyes caught something. A man across the small crowd wearing a Langichatte t-shirt.

Twitchy Forkan: "The man on that t-shirt do you know him?"

Villager: "Do I know him? Everyone knows him. He's Haiti's hero."

The Twitchy Forkan clutched his chest. Gasped. His eyes went wide with the electric joy of cosmic coincidence aligning.

Twitchy Forkan: "Look at God. This is exactly the man I want to visit! (grabbing the villager's shoulders) where can I find him?"

Villager prying to himself, why is this man acting a little strange? Hold back a bit then answered. "He's in Haiti right now. I don't know exactly where, but I know the address of the police station he works out of. You want me to write it down?"

Twitchy Forkan straightened to his full, soaking-wet height. Nodded with the gravity of a man receiving scripture. "Yes. Can you kindly?"

The villager pulled out a scrap of paper, scribbled directions, and handed it over. Twitchy Forkan held it aloft like a holy artifact, eyes wild, suit still dripping, grin twitching. Dramatically turn towards the sun while laughing. The paper fluttering in his hand like a flag from an army of one. "At last. My friend. I'm going to pay you back."

❖ ❖ ❖

to be continued

Agent 009 Langichatte Labond will return.